PRAISE FOR
THE ARMY BRAT HAUNTINGS

"Cary Herwig's *The World Ends at the River* perfectly captures the languid summer days in the South of the 1950s. You feel the sticky heat, hear the drone of bees, see the lightning bugs at night...and you also feel deeply for the protagonist, a young girl on the verge of womanhood who discovers her family's unearthly inheritance and the consequences that it brings I kept turning page after page... and I will be waiting eagerly for the next installment. Highly recommended."

— KATHRYN PTACEK, AUTHOR OF *SHADOWEYES* AND EDITOR OF *WOMEN OF DARKNESS*

"*The Ghost''s Daughter* by Cary Herwig is a suspense-filled novel that held my attention throughout. This novel took me back to the 1950s when society expected women to be seen and not heard... I loved Vivien's courage and dedication to her family. Thank you for this captivating story."

— JENNIFER IBIAM, *READERS' FAVORITE*

"Hysteria. What else could it be? At Camp Breckenridge in 1956, Vivien is continually drawn to an abandoned hospital where she encounters something bizarre and terrifying. This book pulled me back to a simpler time and kept me on the edge of my seat. The characters were lifelike and the danger was real. It kept me turning the pages to find out what happens next."

— BETSEY KULAKOWSKI, AUTHOR OF THE VERITAS CODEX SERIES (FOR *THE GHOST'S DAUGHTER*)

GAME OF THE DEAD
THE ARMY BRAT HAUNTINGS
BOOK FOUR

CARY OSBORNE

To Bryan
Happy 4th!
Cary Herwig

Copyright © 2024 by Cary Osborne

All rights reserved.

No part of this book may be reproduced in any form or by any electronic or mechanical means, including information storage and retrieval systems, without written permission from the author, except for the use of brief quotations in a book review.

CHAPTER ONE

FT. HOOD, TEXAS
JUNE 8, 1960

Brambles pulled at Vivien Brewer's jeans and tried to trip her. Why did she like hiking out here on the Ft. Hood reservation so much when it was such a struggle? More of a thicket than a forest, the density limited her field of vision and she'd lost sight of Daddy. With few exceptions, most trees were no bigger around than her index finger. Hard to believe the city of Killeen lay just a few miles away.

She had not inherited her father's sense of direction, and she relied on him when they spent time hiking in the wilderness that belonged to the U.S. Army. She only had to shout, and he would find her.

She tripped and fell to one knee. Vines and brambles tangled around her foot, preventing her from moving. She pulled at the tangle trying not to be stuck by the thorns. They couldn't penetrate the leather boots, but the vines tightened their hold as she struggled.

Little sunshine reached the floor of the thicket, the shadows making it hard to deal with the tangle. "Ouch!" One of the brambles stuck her finger. She managed to stand and balanced on one foot while she tried to pull her foot free. Suddenly, the tangle broke and she fell backward.

"Shit!"

She'd landed on something hard, and it hurt. She looked around quickly, hoping Daddy hadn't heard her. The chittering and tweeting of birds stopped. She got back to her feet, trying to avoid getting stuck again, and rubbed her butt.

It was still morning but the day had grown hot. In the thicket, the air felt humid and smelled of soil and vegetation. She kicked the ground, looking for the hard something she landed on and discovered a half-buried slab of wood clearly shaped by a human hand. One edge had been squared off, and a whole side looked to have been sanded smooth. Curiosity overcame discomfort, and she knelt down to search the ground for a stick to make it easier to clear away the debris.

The board looked to be about nine inches by twelve and four inches thick. Her fingertips traced letters carved into the smooth surface, which proved not to be as smooth as it looked. She guessed it might be a marker of some sort. Out here, in the middle of nowhere?

Something moved noisily behind her, coming nearer. She turned and recognized Daddy's orange hat. He didn't seem to have spotted her, so she called to him.

He stopped and looked in her direction. "There you are."

"I found something."

"What?" He plowed through the brush and reached her side.

With open space limited by the thick growth, it felt crowded where they stood. Vivien stepped away as best she could and pointed at the ground. "It's some sort of marker, I think."

"Out here?" He stooped down and studied it. He ran his hand over it, slowing when he touched the lettering. "I can't tell what it says."

"Maybe we can move it into the sunlight."

"It's heavy. No idea how deep it's buried."

"We can't leave it here without knowing what it says."

"Of course, we can."

Maybe they should leave it. Maybe even forget about it. A marker could mean a grave, which could also mean a ghost. The ten months they'd been in Texas had been peaceful, the only scary things being high school algebra and home economics. No need to look for trouble. Vivien nodded mentally, knowing all the while her curiosity would not let her walk away.

"Isn't your camera in the truck?" she asked.

"Yes."

"I'll go get it." She looked around. "Which way is it?"

Daddy looked pained when he pointed. "See that grey rock? Walk straight toward it. The road is a few steps beyond. When you get to the road, turn left. The car is about two hundred yards that way. When you come back, look for the rock and head toward it and straight on to me."

Vivien nodded. That should be easy even for her.

CHAPTER TWO

They hadn't set the table when Daddy drove up in the new—to them—1957 Chevrolet 210. They left the 1952 Chevy in France, having sold it to a young soldier, newly arrived at Fontenet. The newer Chevy, an ivory color, four-door sedan, was a step up they could only afford with the money from selling the old one as down payment.

"Hey," he called when he came through the door. He kissed Mama on the cheek and handed the envelope of pictures to Vivien. He got them developed at the Post Exchange, or PX, which cost less and was done faster than in town. She pulled out the five photos they took of the marker. The amount of light had varied with different distances and angles. She hoped they got at least one with a clear view of the inscription.

Vivien sat at the dining table between the living room and kitchen in their new mobile home. No one called them trailers anymore, not since they got bigger and roomier. Their first one, eight feet by thirty feet, had one bedroom and not much of a bathroom. This time, the trailer was twelve feet by sixty feet and had three bedrooms and a decent bathroom. Much roomier, like a real home. She especially liked the teal color of the kitchen appliances.

She needed Mama's magnifying glass to read the inscription and started to look for it. "Move your stuff and set the table," Mama said from the kitchen.

Vivien huffed and gathered up pictures, pen, and lined notebook paper, and carried them to her bedroom. Mama called out the door for Lauren to come and help. Daddy had washed up and already sat at the table. The smell of warm tomatoey spaghetti sauce filled the air.

They sat at the table and helped themselves from the large serving bowl. Chef Boyardee had cleverly created a whole meal in a box with a can of sauce, spaghetti pasta, and a small shaker of parmesan cheese. Mama browned a pound of hamburger meat, added the sauce and, voila! Dinner. A lettuce salad completed the meal. They ate quietly until Mama set butterscotch pudding out as dessert.

Daddy described his day and Mama made sympathetic noises about his frustrations with the captain. Lauren had spent several hours at her friend's house, and Vivien read most of the day, but that was not discussion for the dinner table. After they cleared the table and washed the dishes, Vivien returned the photos and writing material to the table. Having found Mama's magnifying glass, she tried to read the words on the block of wood, comparing one picture with another. A few letters were blurred, either by the age of the wood or the lack of light, although given the context, she could guess what they were. She finally printed the words onto a piece of notebook paper from the three-ring binder she used for school.

"Here Lies Florence Macartan
Born Sept 16 1894 – Died June 15 1910
She Did Not Finish"

She sat back and read it two more times. That didn't tell her much about Florence Macartan, or why she died at age fifteen, the same age as Vivien. Or why someone buried her in the woods instead of in a cemetery in Killeen. What didn't Florence finish? The unique last name might make it easy to find records if she needed to find any, which she didn't plan on doing since telling herself she was through with ghosts. Still, she couldn't stop being curious and wondering what the girl's story might be.

She died so young. How? An accident or illness, most likely. She died too late in history for Indians to have killed her, even if her family farmed the land where they found the gravestone.

She studied the engraving again. Most of the words were legible, yet the letters had not been carved evenly. Whoever did the work had not been an expert.

"Did you figure out anything from the photos?" Daddy asked.

Vivien looked up in surprise, being so engrossed in her own thoughts. "Yeah. It's a grave marker for a girl. I've got her name, birth date, the year she died. It also says, 'She did not finish,' but I don't know what that means."

"It must have been important if they put it on her grave marker," Mama said.

Vivien nodded.

"Are you going to try and find out about her?" Mama asked. She cut her eyes toward Vivien, giving the question more meaning.

"Maybe. I don't know. I'm curious about who she was and what she didn't finish, but —"

"I'll help," Lauren piped up.

"Thanks," Vivien said. "If I decide to check it out."

Vivien returned everything to her room and grabbed her book to sit at the picnic table in the yard. Daddy had cobbled the table together with scrap wood left over from building the porch, and she liked sitting outside, in spite of the heat. Mama said it would get hotter in August. If it did, Vivien would have to read inside since the table sat in full sunlight.

She didn't open the book right away; instead, she studied the land around her. Her immediate surroundings reminded her of the trailer park in Breckinridge, Kentucky, treeless in the immediate vicinity. The differences, however, were greater than the similarities.

Her parents bought the piece of land in Harker Heights in a tract designed for mobile homes. They had to get someone with a backhoe to dig a hole for a septic tank, while water and electricity were installed by the company they bought the land from. Their yard was dirt with a few weeds and would probably stay that way. None of the older places had grass. Trees or bushes were nowhere to be seen except for a large cedar just off the road and beside the driveway, which were also dirt. Dust was a problem inside, and the summer heat, which they experienced for the first time, was already blistering.

The mobile home had no shade, but neither had the trailer in Camp Breckinridge. Daddy promised he would install a water cooler when they could afford it. The temperature inside hadn't dropped below eighty degrees since the end of May, when tornados threatened to appear with each spring storm. So far, they'd been lucky.

She sat on the top of the picnic table and opened the book, *War of the Worlds* by H.G. Wells. A breeze ruffled the pages.

Her mind wandered to the gravestone. Florence Macartan.

Vivien wanted to forget the name, the grave marker, and the curious epitaph. Investigating who the girl was might be enough to bring her ghost. Without the bother of coping with a ghost, Vivien could concentrate on reading and maybe making friends. She missed Mignon, the ghost she helped in

France, who had become her best friend. They talked about everything, especially French history. In the end, she could do without friends like her.

After her first year attending Killeen High School, she hadn't made any friends. Having a friend might have helped keep high school from seeming so intimidating.

Lauren, as usual, had made several friends in elementary school. One, Sylvia Grant, lived in Harker Heights within walking distance. They often played together, usually at Sylvia's house, and went to a movie in town by themselves once.

Vivien concentrated on the book until 7:00, time for *Wagon Train*, one of Daddy's favorite TV programs. Since returning to the States from France, she'd become addicted to watching TV. Mama had decided to limit her and Lauren's TV time to two hours on weeknights, a couple of cartoons Saturday morning, and three hours on weekend nights. A few shows she wouldn't miss for anything, and during the summer, when the networks broadcast replacement shows, new favorites must be chosen.

She went inside and poured herself a glass of iced tea. Daddy sat in front of the TV, spit shining his boots. Theme music for the show came on, and everyone took their seats. Vivien became engrossed in the show, unaware of the others, until the first commercial break. A coffin appeared on the screen. A girl's voice spoke.

"Do you ever wonder how someone died when you see a tombstone and read the epitaph? If the person was young, do you feel sad for a life cut short?"

Vivien looked at the faces of her family. Mama crocheted. Daddy brushed his boots. Lauren drank tea.

She looked back at the TV to see a commercial for Chevrolet. She blinked rapidly. Her ghost hiatus might be over.

Why couldn't ghosts simply come out and say what they

want? Why all of the games and hints? Vivien lay in bed that night, replaying the girl's words in her head. Clearly, a challenge to find out the meaning of the inscription.

Of course, she could have imagined it. It was only a voice, after all. And a picture.

There had to be a connection to the grave marker. Too much to be a coincidence, otherwise.

She'd do some checking. Tomorrow, she'd go into Killeen and visit the *Killeen Daily Herald* office to see if they had back issues.

CHAPTER
THREE

Vivien jumped out of the way of the spinning dirt devil. It meandered along the dirt shoulder alongside Highway 190, heading toward town. The hot breeze didn't cool her as it brushed against her bare skin. Mama didn't like for her to go out in public in shorts and halter top, which Vivien preferred. Today, she wore a light sundress with spaghetti straps, which would have been cooler without the half slip under it. Mama insisted so no one could see through the skirt.

The Greyhound bus appeared in the distance to her left, coming from Belton. It ran every hour from Killeen to Belton to Temple, and back. Her parents allowed her to go into town on her own, although Daddy cautioned her to avoid young soldiers on the prowl.

"They have one thing on their minds," he said.

Vivien believed some of them could be trusted. After all, she had met several very nice young soldiers in Breckinridge, particularly Walt, the lifeguard at the pool in the trailer park, and Robert Ackerman, whom she met at the bowling alley in

Fontenet. They'd both been kind to her. Of course, there must be some bad apples in the barrel, but she'd yet to meet one.

The bus stopped and she climbed in, breathing in the cooler air. It might be a local bus, but it was air conditioned. She gave the driver the correct change. The seat behind him was free and she swung into it, hanging onto the metal pole. Although she'd seen the driver once before when she rode into town, they hadn't yet struck up a conversation.

The ride was short, and the passengers disembarked at the bus station on Avenue C. She'd checked the phonebook for the address of the newspaper office. Heading toward Avenue A, she walked too fast at first. The heat didn't allow for much exertion, especially for one just getting used to it. Asnieres-la-giraud, her last home, had more reasonable temperatures.

Her right hand got sweaty, and the clutch purse slipped from her grip. She shifted it to the other hand. By the time she reached her destination, she'd shifted the purse three times.

She pushed open the door and immediately felt cooler once out of the sun. An overhead fan stirred up a slight breeze that helped. She stood still, enjoying the cooler air.

"May I help you?"

Vivien looked around to the woman standing behind a counter. Vivien smiled and walked to the desk. The woman didn't return the smile, which made Vivien nervous.

"Hi. My name is Vivien Brewer. I would like to see old papers for June and July 1910 if you have them."

"Of course, we have them," the woman said. "Why do you want to see them?"

"I'm a sophomore in the coming school year, and my history teacher will require an essay on local history." She'd used the same excuse before when searching the past. It might even be true for all she knew. "I thought I'd get a head start."

The woman stared at her another moment, making Vivien

wonder if she'd had trouble with kids in the past. Maybe she was suspicious by nature or hard of hearing. The woman nodded and did something on the desk, hidden by the counter. In another moment, she held up a set of keys and motioned for Vivien to follow her. She walked toward a doorway behind the desk. Vivien pushed through the swinging gate and followed.

The woman led her down a long hall. She unlocked a door at the end on the right and turned on the light. Unlike the archive at the Manchester newspaper, this room had high windows letting light in. The shelves and windows had been arranged so that sunlight never touched the shelves where large binders sat. The room smelled of neither dust nor mildew. Someone must clean it regularly.

The woman pulled a binder from a shelf and set it on the table in the middle of the room. "Back that far, the paper was called *The Killeen Herald* and only published weekly," she said. "Third quarter," she added with her hand on one binder. "You have something to take notes with?"

Vivien nodded and said, "Thank you."

"I'll check on you in a little while." The woman walked away, leaving the door open.

The room felt stuffy in spite of the cleanliness. A fan probably wouldn't be a good idea since it would ruffle the newsprint, perhaps damaging the pages.

She took her ballpoint pen and writing pad from her purse. The pen had been a gift for her eighth-grade graduation, and she treasured it for that reason and because it was her first ballpoint pen.

She opened the binder and checked the date to be sure. Since Florence Macartan died that month, she might find everything she needed there.

She started with the week beginning Monday, June 6, intending to look through all four weekly issues. The first announced the tournament to begin on Thursday. The next Monday's issue had the article she was looking for on page two. A headline read, "Winning chess player disappears."

Florence Macartan, the only young woman to play in the Killeen Chess Tournament, has disappeared. Miss Macartan had shown great talent, winning her first five games. This week, she played Phillip Nolen in the semifinal match and defeated him in a tight game.

The inscription on the marker read, "She didn't finish." Did those words refer to the final game in the chess tournament?

Vivien turned to the week before. On the front page: "Killeen Chess Tournament." In the second paragraph she read:

For the first time, a young woman has entered the tournament to begin Friday. Florence Macartan's presence has caused a certain amount of discomfort among the other players. Wilbur Foxe, last year's winner, was not pleased with the judges' decision to let Miss Macartan join the men in the tournament.

The article went on to quote Mr. Foxe's words of displeasure.

This young woman is not a worthy adversary for any of the other contestants. Her presence will be a distraction.

He added that he felt certain she would not withstand the strain of competition.

The article added a statement from Miss Macartan saying she welcomed the competition and she was perfectly able to compete with the men. All of the men seemed to have felt the same as Mr. Foxe.

Vivien scanned all of the June issues, hoping for information that might help her figure out what happened. She found details of the tournament. Apparently, Florence had beaten her opponents easily in the first games, and some believed she might actually win the championship. The winner would go on to compete in the Texas state championship in Austin. The winner there would go on to compete in the national tournament.

However, other players interviewed for the article expressed doubts about how she won. Their animosity toward Florence was plain to see. "No girl or woman has ever played in a major tournament, much less won." "She shouldn't be allowed to play." "This is a game for men."

If Florence had won and gone to the state tournament, those men would have been beside themselves. Especially Wilbur Foxe, it seemed. He fully expected to win and made clear that beating a woman to get to the state tournament diminished the achievement.

Would Florence have beaten Foxe? Would she have gone all the way? More importantly, did someone kill her to make sure she didn't win?

Having disappeared for whatever reason, could Florence be a restless ghost, *not* looking to identify her killer or for vengeance, but wanting to finish what she started? In Vivien's first two encounters, the ghosts wanted her to solve their problems. However, Mignon in France wanted something very different: she'd wanted Vivien to stay with her forever. If Florence wanted something, it might only be to finish the game.

She shouldn't be thinking that. No ghost had appeared, not Florence Macartan or anyone else. Her own thoughts might summon her, and that was the last thing Vivien wanted.

CHAPTER
FOUR

Vivien looked further to see what else might have been reported. It turned out the tournament was delayed while the police investigated Florence's disappearance. Her family had no idea what happened to her. The other players declared she became embarrassed because she knew she would lose and scampered off. They generally agreed she was in hiding and would reappear after the tournament ended.

The week after the last games should have been played, the tournament continued with the final game. The player Florence beat in the semi-final game, Phillip Nolen, lost to Foxe.

In the interview published afterward, Foxe couldn't hide his exultation. He also couldn't help adding his disdain for a girl trying to compete with men.

Foxe went on to Austin a month later to compete in the state tournament. A man from Orange, Texas, named Oliver Bennett, beat him in the third round.

A later article quoted Florence's family's reaction and plea for information on her whereabouts. Her father stated proudly that Florence would never run away from any challenge, much less a chess game. "She was proud of her ability to play chess," he stated. The police claimed to have found no information and considered the case closed. Vivien found nothing else on an official investigation or speculation as to where the girl might be. She would have liked to see a picture of Florence, but no such luck.

Vivien closed the binders and left the room, turning off the light and closing the door behind her. She felt anger on Florence's behalf at the attitude of the men against whom she competed. It was a game, for God's sake. Sure, the winner got bragging rights and got to stand on the top of the hill for a while. In the end, neither winning nor losing could be considered a life-changing event. In her opinion.

She walked down the hall toward the front desk, her thoughts and emotions churning. Yes, chess was a game. Yes, mostly men played. Whose fault was that? She suffered another moment of the unfair treatment of women.

About the same time, she had her first menstrual period at age eleven, her mother sat her down and explained a few facts of life about being a woman. "It isn't always fair," she said. "Men expect us to bend to their will, accept them as our bosses and our children's, and we're supposed to do all the child rearing."

At the time, Vivien figured it had always been that way, so why worry about it? She did most of what she wanted, although she had balked at some rules she and all women and girls had to follow, especially as military dependents, like always wearing dresses or skirts on post. She'd even heard someone say—she couldn't remember who—that the military allowed families to join their men in overseas assignments so the soldiers would be content.

By the time she stopped at the front desk, Vivien wondered about her own father. She loved him dearly, even though he clearly believed women had their place and men had theirs. She'd heard him criticize women for not doing as their husbands said, for dressing in a way he called provocative, for talking loudly or behaving unladylike. Part of her wanted to behave in a way to gain his approval, yet she chafed at the restrictions.

She told the lady at the desk she'd finished in the archives and thanked her. She walked out, blinking in the bright sunlight. She continued wondering about Daddy. What would he think if she challenged men in what they considered their own game? Would he stop loving her?

Sadness at the possibility consumed her as she made her way home. She still worried over the questions when she walked into the trailer. Mama asked, "Find what you wanted?"

"Pretty much."

Vivien started toward her bedroom, but Mama stopped her. "What's the matter?"

"Nothing."

"You sound like you've lost your best friend." Mama drew her to the kitchen table, and they sat down. "Did you learn something upsetting? Is there a ghost?"

Vivien smiled. "Not yet. It's the grave marker I found. I wanted to see if I could find out anything about the girl."

"And?"

"Mama, do men hate women?"

Mama sat back. "Why in the world would you ask that?"

"I looked up Florence Macartan in the newspaper." She could talk about it since no ghost had appeared for sure. She told Mama about the chess tournament and how angry the men were about having to play against a girl. "They talked so mean about her."

"Being a woman isn't easy, then or now," Mama said. "Men, or most of them, believe women have their place in the world and men have theirs and nothing changes that." Just what Vivien had remembered hearing before. "Women wash, cook, and take care of the children. Men work and shine their boots."

Vivien smiled, remembering the many times she watched Daddy spit shine his boots and polish the brass for his uniform. The polish stunk up the house and she was glad she didn't have to fool with that. But shouldn't she be able to do it if she wanted to? "Has it always been that way?"

"I don't know about always. In my mama's day and her mama's day—yeah, that's how it's been."

After washing her face and hands, Vivien helped set the table and get everything ready for dinner. Lauren came home from her friend's house minutes before Daddy arrived. While they ate, Vivien watched her father. He loved her, she knew. If she wanted to do something—a job, a game, a hobby—considered to be men's territory, would he be angry? Would he disown her?

She remembered the quote from Florence's father. He had been proud of his daughter's love of playing chess and being good at it. However, it seemed most men would condemn any woman who didn't fit their idea of knowing her place.

Her mind rebelled at being pre-judged and having her adult life pre-planned for her. Somehow, with or without her father's approval, she would strive to be whatever she finally decided she wanted to be.

CHAPTER
FIVE

Since moving to Texas, Vivien had continued her habit of taking walks. She'd found it a good way to become familiar with where she lived, from the geography to the ambience, which changed with the seasons. Just as in Asnieres-la-Giraud, she walked mostly on weekends during the school year. Going to school in Killeen meant she and Lauren rode the school bus into town each morning and back home in the afternoon. As soon as they got home, the two of them did homework and set the table for dinner.

When spring came, the days lengthened and grew warmer, bringing violent thunderstorms and the beginning of tornado season. This year, there'd been no twisters in central Texas, and now, in June, the winds might blow, but they were nothing to worry about.

In Texas summer heat, she'd changed her walking habits. Rarely an early riser, she'd begun waking up around seven o'clock in the cooler mornings. As summer season went on, the morning temperatures stayed in the low eighties. She could handle that.

First, she explored the trailer community where she lived. The streets were dirt and named after members of the Harker family, who had owned the land. Brushing dust from her body and clothes became a regular routine, whether the wind rose or not, sometimes raised by each step she took. Mama insisted she wear a hat in the sun after her nose got terribly sunburned after all the hours spent in the pool in Breckinridge.

It also became her responsibility to get the mail from their rural box out on Highway 190 after school let out for the summer. The mailboxes sat in a row three blocks from home on the opposite side of the highway. It was also where she caught the Greyhound bus into Killeen.

Sometimes, she walked up and down the highway, seeing where others lived and worked in Harker Heights. Slightly undulating, the highway stretched a long way in either direction. No trees broke up the view. Another large, well-established trailer park sat to the north on the opposite side of the highway. On the near side of the highway, a gas station and small store sat on opposite corners of Harley Drive, the dirt road leading toward her home. Students living in the area caught the school bus into Killeen each morning in the parking lot of the grocery store.

Most of Killeen's streets remained a mystery, although her trips to the library, and now the newspaper office, gave her the opportunity to explore them. She and Lauren went to the library on their own every other Wednesday to pick up their week's supply of reading material.

As spring hurried into summer, the heat, even in the morning, became too much for her. Even her fair complexion tanned during her walks. She'd learned in Breckinridge when she and Lauren spent hours at the pool that she burned easily, so it was best to expose herself to the sun in small bits of time at first. Wince the sun's rays beat down intensely in Central Texas, she'd started slowly in the morning walks, and only for an hour or less in the beginning. She and Lauren both longed to go swimming, but the city pool in Killeen cost money. Vivien thought of asking Mama if they could live with Grandma in summer, where they could go swimming in the ford. She hadn't worked up the courage.

Television helped the boredom in the evenings. The worst of that came at 6:00, Saturday nights, when Mama insisted on watching *The Lawrence Welk Show*. She loved his "champagne music," and Vivien hated it. Books came in very handy on those evenings. That and watching the stars while lying on the picnic table.

Without much else to keep her busy, Vivien thought of Mignon more and more. The young French girl's ghost had been dangerous. She'd wanted Vivien to stay with her, which meant having to die. Even if that prospect had been attractive, Mignon already had half a dozen or more companions whose life energy she'd sucked out to keep herself strong.

Many times they'd walked and talked together, shared who they were. They'd bonded, something she'd never experienced with anyone other than her family. They were best friends. She'd never had a best friend before and the loss lay like a stone in the pit of her stomach every time the memories reminded her. Which was often when the days of no school ran together.

Vivien checked the calendar hanging in the kitchen. Wednesday and too late in the day to go to the library or the newspaper office. She wasn't sure more information about Florence could be gleaned from the back issues of the newspaper. Even the information she'd already found had lost its appeal. Could it be the only people in the past who interested her were those whose ghosts came to her in need of help of some kind?

She slammed the book shut and left the trailer. Hoping for a ghost to appear was all wrong. She wasn't hoping for Florence's ghost to walk up to her and say . . . what? I'm unhappy? Find my family? Find out what happened to me or why it happened?

Daddy came home, and the routine of dinner and cleaning up the kitchen distracted her from gloomy thoughts. Darkness fell, and she went outside to sit at the picnic table. The family watched *The Price Is Right*. She didn't care for game shows and would have preferred to watch *Men Into Space*, but she was outvoted. She lay down on the tabletop and stared up at the stars. The Milky Way spread across the sky.

She held her breath and made a wish when a falling star streaked across the darkness overhead, one of the brightest she'd ever seen. Was it really a star or some heavenly debris? Maybe it was time to get a book on science at the library next time.

"Beautiful," a voice said close to her.

Thinking it was either Mama or Lauren, Vivien glanced over. She sat bolt upright and slid to the ground.

"Who are you?" Vivien's mind rebelled at who the girl standing close might be.

"You know who I am."

"No, I really don't."

Vivien could guess. Another ghost. She didn't want to know. Why couldn't they leave her alone?

"Please go away."

"I can't do that. You have been looking for me." The ghost spoke softly with a strong southern accent.

"I have not."

"Ever since you found my grave marker, you've wondered who I am, what I want. What does 'she didn't finish' mean?"

Panic choked Vivien and she panted for air. "I can't do this. Not again."

"I need —"

"I don't care what you need. Find someone else."

"I've waited so long." The girl looked down at her hands and held palms up in front of her. "I guess I can wait."

"I'm sorry."

The girl disappeared in an instant. Most other ghosts had faded from sight, but Florence didn't waste any time. Vivien almost heard the "pop."

Vivien looked around, making sure the ghost hadn't moved nearby to lurk behind the shed or in deeper shadow. All she remembered of the girl's appearance was a large bow in her hair and she was about Vivien's age.

Lights shone in the neighbor's trailer to the right. A young couple had moved into the trailer several days after her family. Mama met them soon after. She told the girls to stay away from them. She didn't say why at the time, however, Vivien overheard Mama tell Daddy the newcomers were "white trash."

Mama's use of the term shocked Vivien. She rarely spoke against people, although she could make clear what she thought of someone with a single glance. This couple must really be beyond the pale.

At that moment, shouting came from inside the trailer, a man and woman. A loud crack and a woman's voice cried out, followed by a moan. The door opened, and the man stepped outside and strode to the pickup. The starter ground, the motor caught, and the lights came on while he backed into the street. Tires spun in the dirt road, raising dust that hung in the air, lit by starlight.

Crying continued, growing softer until Vivien could no

longer hear it. She went inside and the theme music played as *The Price Is Right* ended.

CHAPTER SIX

The whine of the Hoover Constellation vacuum cleaner wound down. The round body settled to the floor. Its floating above the floor on its own exhaust ceased to be fun some time ago, in spite of its futuristic appearance and operation. After a couple of years, vacuuming had become work.

Vivien unplugged the machine and wound the cord. Lauren dried the last of the breakfast dishes and went outside to wait for her friend, Sylvia. Vivien went into her bedroom and got her book. She settled onto the sofa under the front window to read but sat staring ahead without moving for some minutes.

The sounds from the next door trailer last night echoed in her mind. She'd heard about abusive husbands. She'd never seen Daddy raise a hand to Mama. What made the difference between one couple and another?

"Something on your mind?" Mama sat at the dining table. How long she'd been there, Vivien couldn't guess.

"Daddy hasn't ever hit you, has he?"

"Of course not. Why do you ask such a question?"

"Last night, when I was sitting out on the picnic table. I heard the guy next door hit his wife. She cried."

"I suspected he probably hit her."

Vivien frowned, wrinkling her forehead in the way Mama always fussed about. "Why would she let him?"

"Sometimes women don't have a choice."

"That can't be right."

"Husbands have the right to discipline their wives in most states," Mama said. "Maybe all of them." She shrugged. "If a woman tried to have him arrested, ran away, or hit back, she's the one the law will punish."

"Really?"

"Women—wives—aren't always treated fairly."

Vivien remembered her mother saying much the same thing before. "I'm not getting married. I won't let any man hit me. Daddy spanks me sometimes, but no other man will ever hit me."

"I hope not," Mama said.

"We can't do anything to help the woman next door?"

"No. Interfering in someone else's marriage isn't allowed."

"And he can do whatever he wants."

"Yep."

Mama got up and took out a small roast from the refrigerator to prepare for dinner. Vivien looked over at the neighbor's trailer. The heat of rage built inside her. She meant what she said. She'd never let a man hit her.

She opened the book and read for a few minutes. When she looked up, she saw the woman come out of the trailer next door. Even at that distance Vivien could see a dark bruise on her cheek, where she stood on the small wood porch and shook out a rug. Dust scattered by the hot wind rose in the air.

The woman looked young and plain with medium brown

hair covered by a bandana. What could such a small woman do to make her husband so mad he'd hit her?

She gathered the rug back up and opened the screen door. She stopped in mid-stride and looked toward Vivien's trailer. Vivien felt seen, even though she couldn't possibly see into the window. Vivien looked away, and when she looked back, the woman had gone inside and shut the door.

If only she could help the woman. Would a man who hit his wife also hit a nosy neighbor?

Vivien stopped going outside at night to look at the stars and enjoy the quiet. If more violence occurred next door, she didn't want to know. Angry about anything that made her feel helpless, she could do nothing to help the young woman.

A few days later, she spied the woman outside hanging up clothes and, without thinking, she went to the fence. "Hi, I'm Vivien. I live next door to you."

"Hi," the woman said around a clothespin held in her mouth.

Vivien waited for the woman to give her name. When she didn't, Vivien asked, "How long have you lived here?" She knew but couldn't think of anything else to say.

"Just a little while." The woman kept shaking out clothes and pinning them to the line.

"We moved in a few months ago. Do you like it here?"

"It's okay."

"Your husband is stationed at Ft. Hood?" Vivien saw him in fatigues once when he came home in the afternoon.

"Yes."

Vivien felt at a loss on how to continue the conversation. She'd decided if she couldn't keep the husband from hitting his wife, she could at least be her friend, give her someone to talk to.

"Listen..."

The woman picked up the clothes basket and rushed toward her front door.

"See ya," Vivien said.

She acted like she was afraid.

Two days later, Vivien tried again. This time, the woman was digging in a small flower bed she'd started. The ground was hard, and it was tough going. When she'd been out there for a while, Vivien poured a glass of iced tea and carried it to the fence.

"Would you like some tea?"

She wore a sleeveless blouse and shorts, and Vivien saw a bruise on the woman's upper arm. The woman stood and wiped sweat from her forehead with the back of her gloved hand. She hesitated, then said, "Thanks," and approached the fence. Vivien held out the large Tupperware glass.

"That's a bad bruise on your arm," Vivien said.

The woman lowered the glass and her face reddened.

"If you ever want to talk to someone —"

"Vivien," Mama's voice called. "You need to finish your chores."

The woman held out the nearly full glass.

"Finish it," Vivien said. "I'll come after it tomorrow." She turned toward home. "I still don't know your name," she said, looking over her shoulder.

"Bonnie Kaye."

"Bye, Bonnie Kaye."

Vivien skipped to the trailer. Mama waited inside, hands on hips.

"I told you, no interfering in someone's marriage."

"I'm not interfering. I just gave her some of your iced tea and told her if she ever needs someone to talk to —"

"Stay out of it. You'll cause only trouble if you get involved."

Next morning, Lauren and Vivien headed to the library and walked past the neighbor's yard on their way to catch the bus into town. The pink Tupperware glass lay in the yard. When they came home, Vivien retrieved it.

Bonnie Kaye didn't appear outside again for nearly a week.

∽

Vivien slipped out of bed and padded to the bathroom in her bare feet. At one a.m., the temperature inside was still over eighty degrees. Everyone else slept, so she opened the door as quietly as she could and stepped out onto the porch. The air felt slightly cooler and the breeze helped. She started down the steps toward the picnic table when movement caught her eye. The neighbor's door opened quietly and a figure stepped out. Vivien recognized Bonnie Kaye immediately.

Vivien ran to the fence and called out "Bonnie Kaye." The poor woman nearly shrieked in fear.

"Are you running away?" Vivien asked.

Bonnie Kaye neared the fence and nodded. "He'll kill me some day if I don't."

"Where will you go?"

"Wherever twenty dollars will take me."

"Wait," Vivien said and crept back inside.

In her bedroom, she opened the top drawer of her dresser and opened the velvet box she kept her money in. She pulled out a bill, hoping it was the five dollar bill rather than the one dollar, and hurried back outside, afraid the woman may have gone. Vivien ran to her, relieved to see her still at the fence.

"Here," she whispered. "This will help."

"I can't take your money."

"You can if I offer it. Take it and get away."

Bonnie Kaye held the bill to her chest. When she spoke, her voice caught. "Thank you."

"Go."

CHAPTER
SEVEN

"You brat! Stay right where you are."

Vivien looked up from the book to see Bonnie Kaye's husband run out of his yard and come to the gate. He shoved it open and came at her.

"You got my wife to leave me, didn't you, you little bitch."

Before Vivien could say anything, he grabbed her arm in a vise grip.

"I'll teach you to come between a man and his woman."

His free hand rose. He stood with his hand raised, struggling to bring it down. Florence's ghost took form behind him, her hand gripping his wrist. From his terrified expression, he had no idea what had happened. He yelped and struggled to free the hand, finally releasing his hold on Vivien's wrist. The ghost threw him to the ground in a maneuver Vivien had seen wrestlers use on TV.

"How'd you ... What ..." he sputtered.

Mama burst from the trailer and came at the man with the old baseball bat belonging to the girls. "Get away from my daughter," she yelled. The look in her eyes would kill him if the bat didn't.

He scrabbled to his feet and ran out of the yard and back into his own. "Witch!" he yelled from his yard, and almost leapt into his trailer, slamming the door behind him.

Mama wrapped her arms around Vivien and held her close. "Are you all right?"

"I'm fine."

"I told you not to meddle." Mama drew her inside and picked up the telephone.

"Are you calling the police?"

"No," Mama answered. "I'm calling your father."

Vivien dropped onto the sofa and tried to slow her breathing. Between being attacked by Bonnie Kaye's husband and her mother's rage, she felt excited and frightened, all at the same time. Daddy wouldn't be too happy with her, either. She couldn't tell him a ghost saved her.

Daddy got home in less than thirty minutes. "Where is he?" His voice was cold and hard.

"He's gone," Mama said. "Got in his truck and drove as fast as he could."

Daddy went to the sofa and lifted Vivien up by the shoulders. "Did he hurt you?"

"Not much. Just my wrist." She raised her hand so he could see the bruise beginning to color.

"Son-of-a-bitch."

She'd heard her father curse often, but he'd never used that term before, and it shocked her. It calmed her at the same time. Daddy was here, mad, and ready to defend his family.

He stepped to Mama and wrapped his arms around her shoulders. "Are you all right?" His voice was muffled by her hair.

"I'm fine."

"You should have seen her," Vivien said, pride rising in her.

In reality, however, it was Florence who saved her.

For the next few days, they all watched for Bonnie Kaye's husband to return without looking directly at the trailer. Lauren, who was at her friend's house at the time of the excitement, complained of missing out on the fun. Mama and Vivien looked at her like she was crazy.

Florence didn't reappear until three days passed. Vivien had expected her to come immediately, pointing out she was owed by Vivien now. She came when Vivien lay on top of the picnic table watching the stars, thinking deep thoughts. The man from next door hadn't been seen since he drove away.

"What are you thinking about?"

Vivien froze. She sat up slowly and saw the ghost sitting on the bench of the table, her arms crossed on the top. Finally, she'd come to demand the favor.

"I was just watching the stars. I love seeing the ones streaking across."

"Me too. There are a lot right now."

Vivien slid off the top and onto the bench on the opposite side, careful not to pick up a splinter. "I've been looking for you to come."

"Have you?"

"Of course. I knew you would feel I owe you after the other day."

"Maybe. But we also recognize a person who will help us."

"We?"

"I am not alone."

"How many?"

"A few. Most go on. Only a few . . . Well . . ."

"I sort of guessed that." Vivien folded her arms on the table, mimicking Florence's position. "What do you want?"

"I want to finish something. It's important."

"What is it? What could be so important?"

"The chess game."

Vivien straightened and gave the ghost a long look. The girl died at fifteen, possibly violently, and she wanted to finish a chess game. Crazy.

Florence looked up at the sky while Vivien studied her. She wore a tan dress with brown accents. It fit a bit tight, with ruffles edging the high neck and short sleeves. The material looked worn. Her dark hair had been curled and tied back with a large orange bow. She looked prim and proper, if poor.

"A chess tournament, actually," Florence added, still looking up.

"You died before the tournament ended."

"After the semi-final game."

"It was a big deal?" Vivien had never played a game of chess in her life. What she'd seen on TV and once in a park where two old men played looked boring. All the men did was sit and think. Every so often they'd move a piece. Of course, she'd never seen an entire game and didn't know the first thing about tournaments.

"So, someone thought you might win or something?" Vivien asked.

"Yes. I was the only girl. All the other players were boys and men. They didn't appreciate my even being in the tournament, much less beating them."

"Is that why someone killed you? You were winning?" She'd remembered what she'd read about the tournament in the old newspapers. Now she got a stronger sense of how important it had been to the players.

"The next game was for the Killeen championship," Florence replied, avoiding the issue of her death and burial. "The winner went to Austin for the state tournament. That winner went all the way to Chicago. The men in the tournament did not like the idea I might win. Especially Mr. Foxe. He won the year before, then was beaten in Austin."

When she'd first tried to sign up for the tournament, the men had protested loudly, she explained. No woman of any age had ever played in the tournament. None were members of the chess club, they argued. Mr. Foxe argued loudest. More than anyone, he wanted to win and go to Austin again. This time, he'd been heard to say he would win there, too.

"The chairman of the tournament committee felt the same, until he checked the rules.

They found nothing barring women from playing. No one ever considered the possibility of a female chess player. They tried to bully me into withdrawing, but I wouldn't let them make me."

In spite of everyone involved speaking against her being allowed to play, they had to allow her. They mumbled dire consequences. Threats were made. An anonymous letter to the editor of the newspaper described other dire consequences if women were allowed to enter this male-dominated domain. In the end, the men in the tournament promised Florence would be eliminated in the first round, so it didn't matter, anyway.

"But I won," the ghost said. "I even surprised myself. The men insulted the man I beat and me. They insisted I cheated. They shouted promises to beat me in the next round. I won again."

She was supposed to play against Henry Morgan in the second round, until those in charge switched the players and set her against Owen Grant, a much stronger player. She won. Three more rounds and she would make the final one.

"What did your family think?" Vivien asked.

"Mother was furious. Father was proud."

"Why did your mother get mad?"

"No lady competed with men, she said. We might be poor,

but we knew how to behave. I brought shame to the family. Father never said anything to her, but he cheered me on. He promised to buy me a new dress for the final game when I got that far." She smoothed the skirt of her dress with her palms.

"He believed in you."

Florence nodded. "He taught me to play chess when I was very young. He bought me an old book on strategy. It had the moves of some of the most famous games by great players. I played against a few boys in school, but they would not allow me to join their club."

"Did anyone else support you?"

"My little sister. She did not understand the way men fear women becoming too independent. She felt proud of me for winning."

Vivien started to ask another question. Before the words came out, Mama opened the door and called for her to come inside.

"In a minute," Vivien responded. She turned back to ask Florence to come back the next night, but she'd gone.

CHAPTER
EIGHT

Vivien slept little that night. Her mind kept going over what she'd learned about Florence, both from her and in the newspapers. Her admiration for the girl who defied the odds and the tradition surrounding the tournament kept growing. So many things women weren't supposed to do. Her own list grew every day.

The cruel words of the men trying to persuade Florence to quit only made her more determined to participate and, if she set her mind to it, to win. Now, though, would it be possible to help the ghost with her need to play the last game? At the moment, Vivien had no idea how to go about it.

Next morning, Vivien looked through the Killeen/Harker Heights telephone book to see if anyone named Foxe lived in either place. She found no one by that name. She didn't want to ask Mama for help since she wasn't supposed to use their phone.

Any Foxe descendants might live in Belton, Copperas Cove, even all the way to Temple. They might have moved away, but people born in the area rarely moved very far. Even when they went away to college, most of them came back.

If any descendants of Wilbur Foxe still lived in the area, she could check the library for city directories for Killeen and surrounding towns. Wednesday, she would check the directories on her usual visit to the library. This being Monday, the laundry had to be done. Since moving to Texas, Mama had "let" her help with loading the machine and hanging out the clothes to dry. The hot Texas wind made short work of it.

Monday afternoon, Mama sprinkled those clothes needing ironing with a Pepsi bottle filled with water and a sprinkler top. She rolled up the dampened clothes and put them inside old pillowcases, which she put in the refrigerator until the next day.

Ironing commenced early Tuesday morning. Mama slid the iron back and forth on Daddy's shirt and steam rose. She usually didn't wear her glasses because they would steam up and block her vision.

Daddy's fatigues were the most time-consuming. He liked them well-starched and no wrinkles. Mama took care of those while Vivien pressed the flat pieces: handkerchiefs, pillowcases, sheets, and her own blouses. The chore had been bad enough in France, but the summer heat in Texas made it a misery.

In the afternoon she made a list of names from the phonebook and questions to ask if she should identify Foxe's kinfolk. The temperature rose on the shady side of the trailer to a hundred degrees by one o'clock. Thunderclouds that gathered on the horizon to the north never moved south. They hadn't seen any rain since the first of June, and the ground turned hard and dry with a layer of dust on top.

Mama fixed a cool Waldorf salad for lunch with sweet iced tea.

"I miss Daddy coming home for lunch," Lauren said. Vivien agreed. It had been his habit the summer they lived in Breckinridge, but here and in France they lived too far from post. Odd that she hadn't felt the same in Asnieres.

After they ate, Lauren went to Sylvia's house to play. Her friend's family installed an awning along the length of their trailer in early spring, which made being outside almost tolerable.

Vivien sat on the sofa and read her current fiction choice, *Mara, Daughter of the Nile*. The story of ancient Egyptian culture with espionage and romance intrigued her enough that she thought she might look up books on ancient Egypt. The male protagonist wore an amulet for protection against crocodiles, which was the mode of death predicted for him, and she was curious if that was what people did.

Mara reminded Vivien of Florence—a young woman struggling to be her own person, against others' expectations of what a woman should be and do. If only there was someone to talk to about growing up and not letting the world make her into someone she wasn't. Mama always told her what she should do to grow up and be a lady and find a husband. But what if that wasn't what she wanted? Would Mama understand she didn't want to be pushed into what others preferred her to be? Vivien asked herself a question that never occurred to her before: Was Mama happy with her life?

No one could doubt Mama loved her husband and children. But did she give up dreams of her own to settle into the role of mother and wife?

"Vivien, go get your sister for supper," Mama called from the kitchen.

Vivien had lost track of time. Daddy would be home soon. She dashed outside and down the road, only to see Lauren coming toward her. They walked home together without saying much. They'd become distant with one another since they no longer spent as much time together. Dinner was set out by the time Daddy walked in the door. He gave Mama a kiss on the cheek like always.

Conversation didn't begin until they finished eating and sat drinking second glasses of tea. "We may be put on alert," Daddy said.

"When?" Mama asked.

"Probably by Friday. Krushchev is talking big, maybe trying to influence the elections in November."

Vivien still read the newspapers Daddy brought home and knew that Krushchev, the leader of the Soviet Union, made lots of threats. She also read articles about Senator Kennedy and his campaign for president. TV news had something about him and the upcoming Democratic primary every night. Many Texans didn't approve of him because he was a Catholic. Protestant ministers said he would make decisions for the country based on what the Pope wanted. When she saw Kennedy on TV, she believed in him and clipped articles about his campaign from the papers and magazines. Mama liked him, too, but didn't say she'd vote for him.

Daddy talked mostly about what happened on post. Vivien liked hearing Daddy talk about his day. She also felt guilty when she thought how much more interesting his days were than Mama's.

For the first time, Vivien appreciated how dull her life would be without ghosts appearing to her. They gave her a purpose lacking in Lauren's life and maybe Mama's. Although, twice, the ghosts threatened Lauren to get Vivien to do what they wanted. In the end, her little sister didn't remember anything from those encounters.

Their parents settled in the living room to watch TV news while the girls did the dishes. The two began arguing about

Lauren's borrowing Vivien's hairbrush and not putting it back. Daddy shouted for them to stop it. They finished both the argument and the dishes quietly.

Lauren went into the living room to watch TV, and Vivien went outside. At six-thirty, the day remained hot, and she wished for an awning or beach umbrella to shade the picnic table. She preferred sitting there to dragging one of the metal lawn chairs around to the shady side. The two chairs Daddy bought used reminded her of sitting in the Gypsy camp with Mignon's grandmother while she tried to get information to help ward off her granddaughter's ghost.

She missed so much about living in France, from the wonderful bread to hearing the language. One of her classes the past year was first-year French. She'd tried to sign up for second year French, however the counselor said since she was a freshman, she could only take the first-year class. The only consolation had been in speaking French every day with the teacher. They spoke slightly different dialects, which surprised Vivien. She'd never realized people in different areas of France might speak differently.

After two weeks of the class, Mrs. Collins, the teacher, tried to get her switched to the upper level. Again, the administrator said no. To help Vivien keep up with the language and not lose what she'd learned, she engaged Vivien in conversations while the other students practiced writing out conjugations—I am, you are, etc., which, in French, was *je suis, vous etes*, etc. Mrs. Collins let Vivien help the students with pronunciations, and the two of them spoke only French to each other.

Mrs. Collins lent her books written in French and gave her an occasional magazine, and her skill grew. Each summer, the teacher spent two weeks in France. Vivien longed to go with her, but neither raised the possibility. However, she'd left a number of books for Vivien to read. She read three of them right away and saved the rest for July and August.

Lauren came out and put an end to her thoughts. They threw a baseball back and forth for a while. Mama called Vivien to come in to take her bath. Because the hot water heater only held five gallons, they took turns taking baths. Daddy was on duty every day, so he had to bathe every night. Even in the heat, he liked a hot bath, although he used only enough hot water to take the chill off the cold water.

Vivien used only enough hot water to make the water tepid. They never filled the tub, using just enough to soap up and rinse off. Afterward, she put on her baby doll pajamas and went back outside. The sun had set, and darkness made it unlikely anyone would see her. It was cooler, too. She lay on top of the table to watch the stars as usual.

A soft, shuffling noise caught her attention, and she stayed still. "Florence?"

"Yes."

"I want to help you. I'm just not sure how." Vivien turned her head to see the ghost sitting on the bench.

"Oh, thank you."

"Do you have any ideas?" Vivien asked.

"No. Maybe we can figure something out."

Vivien hoped so.

CHAPTER NINE

The Killeen Public Library resided in a store front on N. Eighth Street, three long blocks from the bus station.

Only a few people were in the library Wednesday morning. The door closed behind Vivien, and she shivered in the coolness. She stopped at the information desk and asked if they had air conditioning.

"Yes," the librarian, Miss Fletcher, said. "We received two large gifts to install it. They finished the work Monday."

Why couldn't someone do the same for the schools? Sitting in hot classrooms trying to learn algebra and history was so hard. Oh, this was lovely. Vivien reminded herself to be grateful.

Lauren led the way to their usual table in the fiction section, and they set their bags on top of it. Lauren immediately disappeared into the stacks. Vivien wanted to find the city directories first. She asked Miss Fletcher, who showed her the shelves in the reference section.

First, she looked through the telephone directories. She found no one named Foxe in Copperas Cove or Temple. In the

Belton directory, however, she found two, and in Killeen, three listings. She suspected all of those listed were related to Wilbur Foxe. It stood to reason.

She copied down the names, addresses and telephone numbers in the bound journal she always carried with her to the library. She'd figure out later how to contact them all to see . . . what? Who might want to play chess with a ghost? Who would even remember the tournament, whether directly or as a family story?

One of the men might be Wilbur Foxe's son or grandson. If so, had he learned to play chess, too? Above all, she wanted to know anything about Florence's disappearance.

She paused in her thinking. Not every descendant of Wilbur Foxe would be male. Would any female descendant be a chess player? Given Wilbur's reaction to Florence, it didn't seem likely.

She put the directories back on the shelves in Reference and began scouring the Boys' Fiction section for science fiction. She found it both funny and maddening that a library would classify the genre for boys. She and Lauren both read a lot of science fiction. She couldn't be too mad about the placement, though. It made finding her favorite books easier. This time, she selected three novels by Ray Bradbury. She had recently discovered his work and enjoyed his stories, especially *The Martian Chronicles*.

The library had no books written in French or textbooks. It did have several histories. She chose two and wanted to check out more, but she and Lauren would have to carry the bag of books to the bus station, then from the highway to home. When she saw Lauren's pile, she had to make her leave some. They would never have made it home with all of them. This was one of the problems with taking the bus instead of Mama driving them.

Both the girls wanted to sit and read in the coolness. Going back out into the heat kept them sitting longer than usual. Still, they couldn't stay all day. They lugged the books to the checkout desk and loaded them into the large canvas bag after Mrs. Fletcher stamped them. They each grabbed a strap and carried it between them out the door and down the street. At each corner, they stopped to switch hands.

They carried the bag the same way from the highway where the bus let them off to the house. They breathed in the heat. The sun burned their skin. They opened the screen door and walked inside. The heat there only felt better because the sun didn't beat against their bare skin.

Next time, I won't forget my hat.

Mama handed each an aluminum glass with iced tea. For several minutes, the only parts of them they moved were their hands lifting the glasses. Eventually, they felt able to remove the books from the bag and put them away in their rooms.

Vivien picked up the journal and looked over the notes she made. Tomorrow, she'd figure out how to call the numbers. Today, nap.

Meanwhile, she must think of how to tell Mama she needed to make those calls without Daddy knowing. Although they had installed a telephone immediately after moving in, Daddy told the girls not to give the number to anyone. He also didn't want them using the phone.

"I can't have you girls tying up the line, talking to your friends all the time. It's for emergencies and for me to get calls from the captain."

Most of the kids she knew in school called each other all the time. No wonder she had no friends. None of them lived in Harker Heights. Lauren didn't know how lucky she was, having her best friend living so close.

Talking Mama into letting her use the phone and not

telling Daddy wouldn't be easy. Mama might understand why but keeping it from Daddy could cause all sorts of problems. Lying to both of them went against the grain. She could tell Mama the truth but lie to Daddy. No, that meant Mama would have to lie to him, too. Best to lie to both. Mama might guess the real reason. After all, she knew about ghosts and Vivien's dealing with them. She'd gone through the same thing herself when young due to the family curse.

Only the girls in the family were affected when they entered puberty, and the current possessor of the curse couldn't be helped by those who came before. Mama and Grandma hadn't explained what would happen if they did help her, but they'd adamantly refused to help in the past. Mama didn't explain the reasons, nor did Hester, the old Roma woman in Asnieres-la-Giraud when Vivien visited her in the camp behind the house. In her mind's eye, she saw the caravans sitting on the hill, smoke swirling into the sky from cookfires burning outside.

Tired from the trip to the library, Vivien decided to wait until tomorrow to talk to Mama. She wanted a clear head, and it was easier to put it off until then.

∽

THE BREAKFAST DISHES had been washed and put away. Mama sat on the sofa repairing the hem on a pair of Lauren's shorts. Lauren had already gone to Sylvia's. Vivien took a deep breath and walked into the living room to stand in front of Mama. She'd been waiting for a good time to ask about using the phone.

"What's up?" Mama asked without looking up.

"I need to use the phone," Vivien blurted out. The words of her carefully planned speech disappeared.

"What for?"

"A school project. For extra credit. Interviews. I need to call —"

"What sort of project?" Mama looked up from her sewing.

"A paper. For history." Vivien took a deep breath. "It's a paper on Killeen history. Or a specific event. I want to find the descendants of people who lived in Killeen in 1910."

"Why that year?"

"It has to do with a chess tournament held in Killeen then. I found the story in the newspaper last week."

"Does it have to do with . . ." Mama looked down and dropped her hands and the sewing into her lap. "I'll have to ask your father."

"No, I —"

"I can't agree without his knowing."

Vivien wanted to argue but thought of nothing to say that might change Mama's mind. What could it hurt to ask? If Daddy said no, she'd find another way.

She thanked Mama and went back to her bedroom. She sat on the edge of her bed and looked over the list of names noted on the tablet. Not only had she written down the names and phone numbers, she'd included the addresses. It should be easy enough to locate each one if she had to visit in person. Who might have a street map of Killeen?

CHAPTER
TEN

Daddy said no to her using the telephone. Mama made Vivien ask him herself, and she let him know she supported their daughter's request. Still, he said no. No surprise, of course. Whether he preferred to keep them isolated from others or believed the phone existed for his personal use, she couldn't say. But he rarely used it. Only one call had ever come from his company commander, telling him to come in early.

That meant visiting the people on the list was the only alternative. Writing letters would be easier, although she doubted any of them would respond. Vivien felt confident before. Now that visiting the Foxes on her list was her only choice, she didn't think she could do it. Meeting strangers was difficult for her. In this case, these people might think her some sort of nutcase, especially if they knew nothing about the chess tournament or Wilbur Foxe. Logically, the individuals must be related, and family stories are shared.

She hated to wait, but Wednesday eventually rolled around. Every night Florence appeared, and they talked at the picnic table. She answered Vivien's questions about the tournament, what the male opponents had said to her face and whispered behind her back. How it felt to win against one after another. She had courage and apparently a great deal of talent.

As for the Foxe descendants, she claimed to know little about them or whether they knew much about Wilbur. Whoever might have an interest in chess or what happened fifty years earlier would be difficult to ascertain. Most ghosts were out of touch with the real world, as opposed to the ghost world, where several of those Vivien encountered seemed to sleep until she came along.

Vivien liked Florence, while at the same time, she held back from getting close. Mignon had made her more wary of trusting the spirits who came to her. They all wanted something from her, Nurse Armstrong in Breckinridge threatened her. Helping Yoshi Narita in Manchester led to an attack by the people responsible for the Japanese girl's death. The encounter with Mignon's desire for Vivien to stay with her forever was the hardest.

So far, the only recent threat came from a wife beater, not from ghosts or killers. Occasionally, she wondered where the young woman had gone. Far enough, she hoped.

Wednesday, Miss Fletcher helped find a good Killeen street map. Foxtail Lane was five blocks south of Highway 190, a long hike from the bus station. Vivien wrote down the directions. Now, all she had to do was decide when to talk to Stewart Foxe. What excuse for coming back into town would work? She still had the paper she was supposed to be writing, requiring more research at the library, of course. The harder part would be telling the Foxes why she wanted to talk with them.

Lauren would be no problem since she preferred spending time with Sylvia these days, and one trip to the library in two weeks sufficed for her. That night, Vivien explained to Floroence what she'd found.

"This Stewart Foxe plays chess?" the ghost asked.

"I don't know. The first thing will be to confirm the names I've found are Wilbur's descendants. Then we find out if they play chess. It may be that none of them do."

"They have to."

"It isn't something a person inherits from their family. Even if one of them plays, they might not be very good."

Florence sighed. "True. I want to play Mr. Foxe himself."

"I don't know how we could arrange that."

"You brought me here. You can do the same for him."

"I've no idea how. If you do, be my guest."

"No. I have no idea."

On Saturday, Vivien told Mama she needed to go to the library to do more research. She and Daddy had become accustomed to her going off by herself and didn't object. "Be careful," he said when she told him where she was going and went back to working on the car.

She caught the bus, and before it turned off of Highway 190 toward the station, she got the driver to let her off. That would save her walking extra blocks, although she'd have to walk all the way to the bus station to get home.

She crossed the highway and pulled the directions she'd copied from her bag. The straw hat she'd remembered to wear kept the sun off her face and the back of her neck, but she sweat against the head band. She took it off and wiped her forehead once while she walked. The house on Foxtail Lane sat back from the street, with a front yard of dirt and a couple of scruffy bushes at each corner of the wide porch. An old GMC pickup sat to one side, looking like it hadn't started in a year or more. Two concrete steps led up to the porch and front door.

Taking a deep breath, she knocked on the wooden frame of

the screen door. It rattled in time with her knocking. She pulled the hat off in the shade of the porch, hoping the headband would dry before she put it on for the return trek.

A woman appeared in the shadows of the hall at the back of the house, looking very dark walking toward the screen. Vivien could see her more clearly when she got close. "What?" she said. She wore cut-off jeans and a button blouse tied in a knot above her waist, exposing her midriff. Seeing her face was impossible through the screen.

"My name is Vivien. I'm looking for Stewart Foxe."

"What for?"

"I'm a student at Killeen High School, and I'm writing a thesis on Killeen history for extra credit next year," Vivien said. "A Mr. Wilbur Foxe won the chess tournament in 1910, and I wondered if . . ." She started to say "your husband," but that might not be the case. "I wondered if Stewart Foxe might be a relative. If he is, I wondered if he could tell me anything about the tournament."

The woman turned her head and called out, "Stewart, there's a girl to see you about your Uncle Wilbur."

"What?" A large man appeared from the back too dark to identify. He lumbered to the door. He was naturally a large man, who'd put on quite a few extra pounds. The woman moved aside, and he took her place. "What about my uncle?" he asked.

"I'm doing research for a thesis for extra credit this coming year in school. I wanted to write about the chess tournament in 1910. I think your uncle won that year."

"Yeah. That year and the year before."

"Could I interview you, find out what you know about it?" Vivien asked.

"How'd you hear about the tournament?"

"I found some articles in the *Killeen Herald*."

"Why did you read articles from that year?"

Vivien paused. She couldn't tell if he asked out of curiosity or suspicion. "I wanted a story from forty or fifty years ago."

He opened the screen door and came out. Vivien stepped back, intimidated by the sudden move and his size. "Yeah, I remember the story. The infamous Florence Macartan." He went to one of the webbed lawn chairs and sat down. "Have a seat."

Vivien sat on the edge of the other chair. He wore Bermuda shorts and a sleeveless t-shirt. His jowly face was pockmarked and had a shadow of a beard. He might be in his thirties, but his age was hard to guess.

"Why infamous Florence Macartan?" She pulled out her journal.

"She wanted to play a man's game. Insisted on it. Who'd she think she was?"

"The article said she disappeared."

"She got scared of losing and ran away, didn't she. Never come back."

"You don't think she might have died or something?"

"The police checked around," he said. "Some people made a big deal about it."

"It was strange, her disappearing like that, with the final game left to play."

"She was afraid to face Uncle Wilbur, wasn't she. No girl can beat a man at chess."

"She'd already beaten four men in the tournament."

He looked at her, his eyes squinting and jaw tight. "You ain't suggesting —"

"Do you know these other names?" she broke in. "Are they related to your Uncle Wilbur?"

His face relaxed slightly, and he took the note she handed to him. "Yeah, Lorenz is his son, and Jakob is Lorenz's son."

"Would they know about the tournament?"

"Course. Old Wilbur bragged about his skill at playing chess. Although, he never won a thing at state. Still, he was right proud of those trophies."

"Does his son still have the trophies?" She looked down at the notes. "Or Jakob? Does he have them?"

"Jakob does, yeah. Right proud of 'em."

Vivien slipped the journal and notes into the bag. "Thanks, Mr. Foxe. I appreciate your talking to me."

"You gonna talk to Loren, too?"

"Yes, I'd like to."

"Tell him I sent you. It'll make him mad." Stewart chuckled.

Vivien thanked him again and stepped off the porch. No way would she tell Lorenz Foxe that Stewart sent her. The last thing she wanted was to make him mad before asking him to play chess against a ghost.

CHAPTER
ELEVEN

Vivien reached the bus station and went inside where it was cool. She usually sat on the bench outside while waiting for her bus to arrive, but she'd gotten very hot on the long walk. She drank from the water fountain and sat near the door. From there, she could see the bus arrive.

She sat with her eyes closed for a few minutes, then made a few more notes in her journal. The bus pulled up at the curb. He went inside the building, and she waited in the coolness of the bus station for him to return. When he did, she followed him up into the bus, sitting in the first row of seats next to the door. A young soldier in civilian clothes boarded and walked toward the back. He looked her over as he passed without saying anything. She could always spot them, even out of uniform.

She rarely saw soldiers on the bus, probably because she rode during the day and on Saturdays. Most soldiers had cars, or she thought they did, although she'd heard lots of soldiers rode the bus in the evening, most heading to Temple, where they could drink in bars. A lot of them got drunk. Mama said they were lonely and unhappy. Daddy said they were stupid young men out to find alcohol and women and ended up in trouble much of the time.

At fifteen, Vivien wasn't above flirting with a nice-looking young man once in a while, but only when other people were around. Other girls her age dated. Daddy said she couldn't until she was at least sixteen. Another year. Since none of the boys in high school paid any attention to her and Daddy said she couldn't date soldiers, she felt doomed.

By the time she got home, lunch was over. Mama fixed her a sandwich and a glass of sweet tea. "Did you get what you needed for your paper?" Mama asked with a look suggesting she suspected Vivien's motives.

"Not everything. There are a couple more people I want to interview."

That night, Florence appeared. Vivien told her about Stewart Foxe and their conversation.

"Now you know who to interview," Florence said.

"Yeah, but Lorenz lives in Belton. And Jakob lives a long way from the bus station."

"You'll think of a way."

Vivien wished she felt that confident. Stewart had surprised her. She'd expected a more sophisticated man, given what she'd read about Wilbur. He'd been a businessman and seemed well-known in the town. He also acted like a bully, especially toward Florence. Stewart hadn't progressed beyond being a bully from what she saw of him, at least in his opinions of uppity women or girls. He hadn't known Florence, of course, and it seemed his uncle's attitude may have been handed down to the next generation.

More and more, Vivien worried about how to call on

Wilbur, get him to rise from the grave so he could play the final game with Florence. She had no idea what made some ghosts appear to her, asking for her help. Only once had she seen a ghost rise from their grave, and that wasn't by choice.

Thank goodness she hadn't given Stewart her full name. He might have had the idea she wanted to accuse his uncle of doing something to Florence. The idea had occurred to her, but she wanted no part in figuring that out. She only wanted to help the ghost play the final game.

When she re-focused on Florence, the ghost was reminiscing aloud about the games she'd played in the tournament. She recalled every move and counter move in each one.

No wonder I can't learn to play. I don't have that kind of memory.

Her mind wandered again, planning her next trek into Killeen. She had to go earlier, when it was cooler. Not that the trailer ever got cool these days. Tomorrow, Sunday, would be better than waiting another week to go next Saturday. Of course, Lorenz and his family, if he had one, might be in church. She'd take that chance.

∽

SUNDAY BREAKFAST DISHES had been cleared, and everyone sat around the living room, reading the papers. Vivien fidgeted. She hadn't come up with a good reason to catch the bus into Killeen this morning. She searched for the crossword puzzle in the *Herald* with only half a mind, until a headline caught her eye: *Chess Tournament to Be Re-enacted.*

The article that followed described the chess tournament of 1910, fifty years ago. It detailed the wins of both Wilbur Foxe and Florence Macartan. It also described Florence's disappearance and speculation about what happened to her. Near the end, it described the final tournament between Foxe and Phillip Nolen.

"The tournament will be dedicated to the memories of all those who played in the 1910 games, especially to Mr. Foxe and Florence Macartan. Miss Macartan participated in spite of barriers put in her way."

The reporter didn't elaborate on what those barriers were. He could mean her lack of talent because she was female, or the attitudes of the men who opposed her, both as opponents at the chess board and as men who disapproved of having to play against a young woman.

Florence must know about the re-enactment. That's why she appeared now. Not because of Vivien's finding the gravestone. That part could be the reason she appeared to Vivien, of course. Vivien skimmed the article to find when and where the games would be played. The week beginning June , essentially the same week as the original tournament, and the games would be played in the auditorium in the old Killeen High School, now Avenue D Elementary School.

Florence not only wanted to play against Wilbur Foxe for the championship, she wanted to play the game exactly fifty years later and in the same venue.

Vivien cut out the article to keep the information. It included a phone number to call if you wanted to volunteer to help with the tournament.

That night, when Florence appeared, Vivien accused her of not being honest. "You knew about the tournament re-enactment, didn't you?"

"Yes, but—"

"If I'm going to help you, you have to be honest with me."

Florence disappeared, leaving Vivien angry and frustrated.

There was one consolation. With Florence disappointing her, she wasn't about to get close to the ghost. Vivien hadn't gotten over Mignon's betrayal. Her first best friend had been more of a false friend than anyone could know. She didn't need another disappointment like that.

CHAPTER
TWELVE

Next day, Vivien asked Daddy to let her use the phone this one time. He said no again. She took a deep breath and tried again.

"Volunteering for a community event will look good on my record when I start job hunting," she said. "Plus, it will keep me busy for part of the summer."

Mama supported her request; he still he wouldn't give in. However, at supper that night, he asked for more information about the tournament. Vivien showed him the article.

"Good sponsors," he mumbled. "You won't have problems getting there when you need to? I'll be at work and won't be able to take you."

"The bus schedule is all right, and the school isn't far from the bus station."

He asked a couple more questions. "All right," he said finally. "It says to call between one o'clock and four. You can use the phone to call tomorrow."

Vivien yelped in surprise and excitement. "Thank you. Thank you."

He kissed her cheek and went into the living room to watch TV. Vivien sat at the dining table with her journal and listed what she wanted to ask about relative to what she'd be doing.

The article said Wilbur Foxe's descendants—son and grandson—would participate in the

tournament. It did not say whether they would actually play any of the games, nor did she yet know if they played chess. Regardless, she would be able to see them in person without having to visit them at home. Could she convince either of them to play against a ghost? They would think her crazy, but if they saw Florence, they would have to believe her.

She couldn't wait to tell the ghost she would be at the tournament. On second thought, she should wait until after she made the phone call.

When Vivien called the number in the article, the woman on the other end, Mrs. and , didn't seem eager about her volunteering once Vivien told her she was a high school student. "Do you play chess?" the woman asked.

"No. I've tried a few times. I can organize things, put out chairs, get food and drink, things like that."

The voice on the other end didn't respond immediately. Vivien pictured a middle-aged woman, greying hair in a bun, glasses, brow furrowed in deep thought. She tried to think of other things to say to convince her, but what could she say? She had little experience with tournaments, chess, or any event planning. She started to say, "I'm quick to learn," but the woman spoke.

"Why don't you come to the school tomorrow and we'll chat. We'll try to work something out."

"What time?"

"After lunch. One o'clock."

"Thank you," Vivien said. "I'll be there."

She felt herself grinning widely when she went to tell Mama.

"Congratulations," Mama said. "Your first job interview."

"Really? I hadn't thought of that."

"I'm proud of you. You'll learn a lot. It should be fun, too."

Surprised, Vivien realized she looked forward to the tournament itself, although she didn't like crowds much. In this case, she guessed the number of people would probably not be large. How many people enjoy watching others sit thinking about where to move little figures on a checkered board?

What she hoped for, however, was to meet and talk with Jakob and Lorenz Foxe. She'd learn pretty quickly if the son and grandson followed in Wilbur's footsteps.

∼

THE BUS REACHED the station at 12:15. It would take ten to fifteen minutes to walk to the school on Avenue D. She checked her wallet and found two dollars. Around the corner was a small café she'd never been in before. She ordered a Cherry Coke from the menu displayed on the wall. She'd been too jittery to eat lunch, and the walk to catch the bus made her thirsty. She guessed the temperature to be in the nineties at least.

She looked down at the light sundress she wore while she waited for her drink. She hadn't worn a dress since the school year ended. It felt odd to have something covering her legs to mid-calf, after wearing shorts every day.

The clock on the wall with the 7Up logo showed twenty minutes to one o'clock. She'd drunk all the Coke and tipped up the glass and got a mouthful of crushed ice. Crunching the ice, she left the café and headed to the school. She went up the stairs to the main door. In the main hall, she stood and looked around. Lauren attended this school last year. Next year, she would move to the junior high school. Vivien had never been inside and had no idea where to go.

A youngish woman came into the hall at the far end. Vivien walked toward her. "Excuse me," she said.

The woman looked younger than Mama, had short blond hair and wore cat-eye glasses.

"I'm here to see Mrs. Stirling."

"You must be Vivien. I'm Mrs. Stirling."

Not at all what Vivien expected.

"If you'll go through the door at the end," she said pointing with a pencil, "I'll be right back."

Vivien nodded and walked to the door, her footsteps echoing in syncopation with Mrs. Stirling's. She pushed the door open and entered the right side of the auditorium. Dozens of folding tables were stacked along the far wall, and chairs sat scattered over half of the space. A smaller table and four chairs sat on the small stage to the far right. A young man sat at a table near the wall on the left side, head down, studying papers spread over a tabletop.

Vivien cleared her throat, and the man looked up, surprised to see someone else in the room. "Can I help you?"

She realized he was younger than she first thought. "Mrs. Stirling told me to wait here for her."

"You must be Vivien."

"Yes."

"Good. We can use the help."

The door opened behind her, and Mrs. Stirling strode in, looking officious. Vivien instantly felt intimidated. If a woman could wear a suit with long sleeves, stockings and high-heeled shoes in this heat, she must be a tough one.

"Jack, do you have the first set of plans for the chairs and tables?"

"Yes, right here." He pulled a sheet from under the rest and glanced at it.

Mrs. Stirling maneuvered around tables and chairs. She took the sheet of paper in a well-manicured hand, looked at it, then at Vivien, and motioned for her to join them.

"Do you think you can sort out this mess according to this drawing?" She indicated tables on the drawing with the pencil.

Rows of rectangles, large and small, represented tables and chairs. Each table had one chair on each side, with large spaces between them.

"Jack will help move the tables into place, evenly spaced, with enough room between them for the judges to walk. The chairs will be left to you. Once they are in place, timers go at each end of every table. They're in boxes on the stage." She stopped and looked over the room a moment. "As each round is finished and players are eliminated, tables will be removed, leaving just enough for the remaining players. Jack is finishing the drawings for each round."

"How many rounds?"

"Six. Sixty-four players to start. During play, you will stand quietly at the drink table on the other side. The players will raise a hand if they need something. Water, ash tray, whatever. Small sandwiches and other snacks will also be set out for when they take their breaks between matches. No food is to be eaten at the tables where they play."

Mrs. Stirling showed her the bathrooms and water fountains. Pitchers of ice water and iced tea would be available while they played. Vivien studied the space. As it was an auditorium, windows sat high, just under the ceiling along the one outside wall on the left. They probably didn't open. Large floor fans stood strategically around the room to keep the air moving. Even with them, though, the room had become stiflingly hot.

"That dress is suitable," Mrs. Stirling said, interrupting Vivien's thoughts. "So, are you up to it?"

"Yeah, I can do this."

"Yes, ma'am," Mrs. Stirling corrected. "Good. Come tomorrow morning. Jack should have the drawings finished, and he and you can move the tables into place. The janitorial staff simply left everything in here since they're on summer vacation." She exhaled sharply. "Wear your shorts or something cooler tomorrow and Wednesday while you move everything around."

With that, Vivien was dismissed for the day.

CHAPTER
THIRTEEN

The auditorium grew swelteringly hot after the first hour. Vivien and Jack sat at one of the tables yet to be moved into place, drinking sodas straight from the bottles. Mrs. Stirling had left a cooler with several bottles of Coke, root beer, and 7Up for them. They had no idea where she rushed off to.

"How many tables are there?" Vivien asked.

"Thirty-two," Jack said. "Two players at each."

"There'll be thirty-two players in the second round, right?"

"Yes."

"So, sixteen tables."

Jack nodded.

After the first day's play, half of the tables would be removed. The other half would be re-shuffled for the remaining players.

"I wonder why they didn't plan this for a cooler time of year," Vivien said. "A long holiday weekend would have worked."

"This is the same time of year they held the original tournament. It's all supposed to be as close to that one as possible. Plus, with summer vacation, the school is empty."

She asked if tournaments had been held since 1910, but he didn't know. She wondered aloud if further tournaments were cancelled due to the disappearance of the only female participant that year, but Jack appeared to know nothing about that history, either. Vivien asked whether she had been the only person to volunteer to help. One other student, a boy, volunteered. Mrs. Stirling found him unsuitable. Jack didn't know why she rejected his help, nor why others in the high school chess club didn't volunteer.

"Maybe everyone is away on vacation," she suggested.

They finished their drinks and got up. They had half of the tables in place but they waited to move the folded chairs until all of the tables were set out.

Vivien heard a sound coming from the stage. She stopped to look for the cause, but no light reached the raised area, neither from the windows nor the few lights turned on overhead. They'd elected to leave half of the lights off in hopes it would help keep the heat down.

She saw nothing in the shadows at first. Then something moved again. She looked at Jack to see if he'd noticed, however, he had walked toward the tables stacked against the folded bleachers. She slowly approached the stage, watching for any other sign that someone was there. Something moved again. It appeared to be a man, hiding toward the back where the shadows were deepest.

"Vivien," Jack called.

The figure faded.

"Sorry." She turned to join him. She took one more look. "I thought I saw someone on the stage."

"Where?"

"At the back. I was sure I saw something move. For a

moment, it looked like a man standing back there, but I guess not."

Jack looked toward the stage for a long moment. He shook his head. "I don't see anything."

"Just my imagination."

They unfolded the legs, locking them in place, then they moved the table into position. Every so often Vivien wiped her hands on her shorts. All of the tables would have to be dusted off before the players took their places. If they got them all set up soon, there might be time to do the dusting this afternoon.

A noise came from the stage, and this time Jack turned to look. One of the two chairs at the small table had been pushed away. Still nothing or no one could be seen.

"This place could be haunted," Jack said with a short laugh.

For a moment, Vivien considered whether he might be right. Perhaps other ghosts occupied the school. It had been built a long time ago and hundreds of students and teachers passed through.

They both watched the stage another moment. When nothing else happened, they returned to the tables. The next time they heard a noise, Jack strode to the stairs on the left side and climbed up to the stage. Vivien stood at the edge, watching him move toward the back. He nearly disappeared in the darkness in spite of her standing so close. He walked from side to side and back to front.

"Nothing," he said.

The door opened, and Mrs. Stirling called out, "What are you doing up there?"

Vivien whirled around, feeling both guilty and startled.

"We heard something up here," Jack said.

"Did you find anything?" Mrs. Stirling asked.

"No, nothing."

"Then get back to work."

They both said, "Yes, ma'am," and returned to setting out the tables.

Mrs. Stirling moved to the table where the drawings lay and looked them over. She picked up the one on top and, looking from it to the room, nodded her satisfaction. "Well done," she said. "I'll be back at four to lock up."

"All right," Jack said and smiled.

Earlier that day, Jack had told Vivien that Mrs. Stirling had been his seventh-grade teacher.

"Did you like her?"

"Yeah, she's a good teacher, although a bit abrupt. That's why I volunteered."

"What year did you graduate?"

Jack laughed. "I graduate next year."

"Oh, I thought you were out of school."

For the next hour, while they worked, they both looked at the stage every so often. They took another break at three o'clock and had another soda. Jack had discovered an ice machine in the small kitchen separated from the auditorium by a door near the back. He added some ice to the cooler, and they put ice into two glasses they also found in the kitchen. They poured soda over the ice and savored the cold, carbonated drinks.

They sat quietly for a while, and Vivien considered what might have made the noises on the stage. She might have seen Florence, except the figure looked more like a man. Why would she, or any other ghost, not stand there silently? Why make noise or move the chair?

If it was another ghost, one possibility was Wilbur Foxe. Would he come back to watch the tournament and relive his triumph?

CHAPTER
FOURTEEN

The bank marquee showed the temperature was already 85 degrees when she passed it on the way to the school. Vivien walked slowly to avoid getting any hotter, not that it helped much. Today's temperature was forecast to be near 100 by the weatherman on TV.

She'd caught the bus at 6:45 to get to the school as early as possible. Some of the timers must be set out, pitchers to fill with ice water, electric fans to turn on, and whatever else they found needed doing. She and Jack would see to all of that and assist the players during the day.

The players were supposed to arrive at 8:30 and play to begin at 9:00. Vivien found it easy to envy their talent, but on such a hot day, concentrating would be hard for all of them.

For setting out name cards, she referred to the chart, while Jack took care of the timers. Mrs. Stirling had rounded up more fans, both table and floor models. Someone had placed them after they left the day before so they either blew up toward the ceiling or down toward the floor, circulating the air while not blowing directly on the tables or players.

Players from Killeen Chess Club, Belton Chess Club, Killeen High School Chess Club, Belton High School Chess Club, and a few from smaller clubs in the surrounding communities had signed up. The color of each card indicated the player's affiliation. The Killeen High School Club included two girls, which Vivien had not known until she began putting out the name cards. That could make the day a little more interesting, although she hoped not in the same way it had in 1910.

A few non-club members were included. Among them, she noticed the name Jakob Foxe. She made a mental note of where he would be sitting.

The pitchers would be filled and the food set out after players arrived. She and Jack were still making final adjustments when Mrs. Stirling walked in. She called for them to get the rest of the grocery bags and drinks out of her car while she dropped the bags in the kitchen. The three carried coolers filled with sodas, bags of chips, and other snacks into the kitchen. Small, wrapped sandwiches already sat in the refrigerator. They set plastic glasses, paper plates, and plastic forks on the refreshment tables.

Vivien and Jack returned to getting everything set out while Mrs. Stirling wandered from table to table, checking each against the diagram. She switched two seatings. "Can't have two from the same club playing each other at the outset."

While these preparations continued, four members of the Killeen Chess Club arrived to set up the boards for the first round.

Players began arriving mere minutes after they finished. As hosts, Mrs. Stirling and Michael Jones, the president of the Killeen Chess club, stood at the door to the auditorium to welcome those arriving. Vivien stood behind the refreshment table in case anyone needed help while Jack led players to their seats.

Across the room, Vivien saw a man giving Jack a hard time. She guessed he didn't like his seat. Jack spoke to Mrs. Stirling, then led her to where the man had been. He had disappeared. Vivien looked away to help a player, and when she turned back to search the crowd for the man, he didn't seem to be there. More players looking for refreshments approached, particularly for something cold to drink, and she pushed the incident out of mind.

Mrs. Stirling checked off the names on her clipboard, nodded, and the doors were closed. She and Mr. Jones went to the stage. She rang the hand bell to announce the tournament was about to begin.

"Welcome, everyone," she said. "Please be seated." Once everyone had found their seats again, she continued, "Mr. Jones and I appreciate your entering the tournament. We want to thank everyone who worked hard to make it happen."

Vivien and Jack looked at each other across the room, smiled, and nodded.

"You will be playing under a modified Swiss system." She explained that the top players of the two city clubs would play each other, the second-ranked players would play, and down the line. The same with the high school clubs. Meanwhile, the names of the unranked players were drawn to determine who played whom. Players who won in the first round would play each other according to ranking in the second round. There was much more, and she tried to explain as simply as possible.

Mrs. Stirling introduced the four judges who now stood to one side. "Each judge has a copy of the rules. Any questions?" She answered a few. "Our two helpers will be available if you need anything. Please hold up your hand. If it's for a rule interpretation, they will notify one of the judges."

The first and second days, they would play two games. The semi-final and final games would be played on Saturday and

Sunday. Everyone settled in with handshakes all around. One player at each table held up their hands hiding a black king in one hand and a white in the other. The opposing player chose one hand. If it was the hand holding the white piece, they played first.

Everyone took their place without a word. The hum of a dozen fans filled the silence. From where they stood, Vivien and Jack had a clear view of most of the players.

"Who was the man you argued with?" Vivien whispered.

"I don't know."

"What was he bothered about?"

"I think he was angry about including girls. He said something about one of them sitting in his place."

Since Jack saw and spoke with the man, he couldn't be Wilbur Foxe. Unless Jack also had the ability to see ghosts.

Vivien looked over the room and located Jakob Foxe. He looked to be in his mid-twenties, and like many of the men, wore his hair in a crewcut. He pushed heavy framed browline glasses up on his nose and concentrated on the pieces on the board. He wasn't the one who argued with Jack earlier, which she thought might have been the case. He'd drawn black and moved second. After each play, he took a drink from the plastic glass. When he'd emptied it, except for the ice, she refilled it. He looked up and nodded a thank you and returned his attention to the board.

Although she did the same for other players, she especially paid attention to Jakob, letting him see her each time. She wanted him to remember her when she approached him later. She intended to wait to approach him after the final game on Sunday.

After half an hour, three games had ended. Those players moved to chairs lining the wall on one side to watch. Jakob won his game soon after and walked away from the table with a self-satisfied look. Vivien quietly congratulated him and the other winners when she passed where they sat, waiting.

The final game ended three minutes past twelve. Jack and Vivien grabbed trash cans and cleared the tables of debris and emptied ash trays for the majority of men who smoked. None of the high school students smoked during the games.

The doors were opened, and most of the fans turned to blow cigarette smoke outside. Jakob joined three other men and went outside, probably to smoke. The room still smelled strongly of it. Other players crowded around the refreshment tables, eating and drinking water or sodas.

The two high school girls stood at one end eating sandwiches and comparing notes. They had won their first games, proving they belonged in the tournament. Yet, every so often, two or three of the men looked over at them while whispering to another, as if discussing their presence in the tournament. If she overheard anyone complaining about the girls' participation, Vivien was prepared to remind them that a girl played in the 1910 tournament, which was in keeping with re-enacting that event.

Play resumed at twelve-thirty. Half of the boards and pieces had been put away during the break, along with the timers. Mrs. Stirling rang the bell and asked the participants to resume their seats according to the name cards. Who played first was chosen at each table and some of the boards were turned.

Vivien and Jack resumed their places from where they could see any players raising their hand or waving to them. More requests to consult judges, get drinks, and empty ash trays occurred than during the first set. These games took longer to play, too. One losing player threw his king at his opponent, hitting him in the shoulder. He stalked out, mumbling under his breath. The opponent sat with mouth open, which turned into a smile.

"Arthur always was a sore loser," he said to everyone. He got up and moved to the chairs along the wall with a fresh soda and a cigarette.

All games ended by 3:30. Jakob won again, meaning Vivien would have to wait to speak with him.

While players milled around for several minutes, Jack and Vivien rearranged the tables according to the third diagram. Food and sodas were put away in the kitchen, water pitchers emptied and turned upside down to dry, and dishes washed. They placed chessboards on each table, leaving the pieces in boxes to be set up by the same men next morning.

After everyone left, Vivien and Jack sat in the extra chairs against the wall, drinking sodas and relaxing a moment. Mrs. Stirling came in, startling them when she called out, "Nice job. Thanks. Now we get to do it all over again tomorrow." She sat beside Jack and lit a cigarette. She looked over the room. "I'll get the fans turned off," she said. "Go home."

Vivien was about to stand up when she saw movement on the stage. She sat still, watching. Again, she saw the figure of a man standing still in the shadows.

CHAPTER
FIFTEEN

Mama had a snack ready for Vivien when she got home. "You had a long day," Mama said. "I didn't know if you'd get lunch or not."

"We had a sandwich and a 7Up," Vivien said. She ate the brownie and sipped the iced tea.

Mama sat at the table, ready to hear about her daughter's very first workday.

Vivien told her about the quiet as the players concentrated on their moves and how everyone smoked, filling the air with smoke. "Some of the men didn't like the two high school girls playing. Both girls won their first round, and one of them won in the second."

"Not surprised," Mama said. She laughed when Vivien described the man throwing his chess piece at his opponent. "Such childish behavior."

Daddy got home at the usual time. He asked how things went at the tournament after dinner when they all sat at the table, drinking iced tea.

"I'm not sure I like your being gone so long," he said. "That's a long day."

"No longer than a day at school," Vivien said.

"I know, but this was a different situation. You're only fifteen. And it is an army town."

"I'm okay. No one bothered me." She couldn't stop now. There was no one else to help with the tournament, and she liked having a job, even if it didn't pay anything.

She told him about the man named Arthur throwing the chess piece, thinking he would laugh. "It was really hot in there and everyone was smoking, making it hard to breathe. Once they opened the doors, though, it got better."

"Sounds like you had a good time," Mama said.

"Yes, ma'am. I felt really grown up."

After a few more comments, her parents went to the living room and turned on the TV. Vivien and Lauren finished cleaning up. She worried that Daddy might not let her go back tomorrow. She'd promised she would be there. It was important to see it through, both as a responsibility she'd accepted and as the best opportunity to talk with Jakob Foxe.

Although it wasn't her night to take a bath, Mama made an exception since she would be working again tomorrow. Afterward, she felt too tired to go outside and look at the stars, which often included Florence appearing. She had little information to share and didn't want to get the ghost's hopes up either. Instead, she got her book and lay on the bed reading until she couldn't keep her eyes open. Mama would wake her tomorrow so she could catch the bus and get to the school on time.

She laid the book aside and turned out the bedside light. In the dark, she tried to plan how to approach Jakob Foxe and what to say. She fell asleep before getting very far.

She dreamed that Florence came to her, demanding she

work faster to set up a game between her and Wilbur. Vivien explained that she couldn't do that and hoped to convince Jakob to take his grandfather's place. None of it made any sense in the dream. When Mama woke her next morning, it still didn't make any sense.

Why would Jakob agree to play against a ghost he couldn't see? She remembered the man in the shadows of the stage, though. Was it Wilbur Foxe's ghost? Was he trying to create more stress? For whom? Could she convince him to play Florence in a final game?

∽

Friday played out much as Thursday had, except on a smaller scale. Fewer players, of course, and several of the eliminated players showed up to watch. Mrs. Stirling said more of them would probably come for the final game.

Jakob won his two games again. She scanned the tables, looking for anyone needing another drink or to have an ash tray emptied. When she glanced over at Jakob, a ghostly figure bent over, whispering in his ear. The figure faded before she could be sure of what she saw. Yet, she accepted that Jakob's grandfather might be helping him to win, whether he knew it or not.

If she was right, perhaps a game between Wilbur and Florence could be arranged. Or, maybe Jakob might be persuaded to play in his grandfather's place. If Wilbur helped his grandson during play, it wouldn't be much different than his playing against Florence, would it?

She'd have to tell Florence tonight what the possibilities might be. That led her to wonder why Florence hadn't appeared at the tournament. Maybe she watched without showing herself. She certainly wasn't the figure in the shadows she'd seen on the stage.

Watching the play yesterday and today, Vivien began to understand some of the strategies and intensity of play. Today, she could see more clenched jaws, more wiping perspiration from foreheads, and "I got you now" looks. The atmosphere on Thursday had been jolly compared to today.

It pleased Vivien that one of the remaining players was also one of the high school girls. She proved women could play as well as most men.

The losing players from the third round moved to the chairs against the wall, joining the players from the day before. When the fourth round ended with the final losing player turning down his king, a collective sigh filled the room. The eight adversaries for the semi-final round looked triumphant and shared handshakes all around, congratulating each other. "Better luck next time," said to today's losers. Jakob was one of the winners.

While the players milled around discussing the individual performances, Vivien and Jack broke down the tables, leaving two for the next day. The players departed slowly; so hyped by the competition, they weren't ready to confront the outside world. It seemed none of them had played for the fun of the game, only for the challenge and the win.

Everything was put away more quickly than the day before, and Vivien rushed to reach the bus station to catch the next bus. If she missed it, she'd have to wait another hour. It pulled up at the same time she went inside to buy her ticket. The driver had gone into the terminal, probably for a bathroom break, and left the bus door closed. She wanted almost desperately to climb inside and sit in the air-conditioned coolness.

When the driver returned, she climbed aboard and took her usual front seat, where she leaned back and closed her eyes. She kept them closed, in part to keep another passenger from wanting to sit next to her. Silently, she counted as the passengers passed by, the sound of each person brushing by as familiar to her as Mama's voice. Some people touched the backs of the seats when they passed. Women passed, leaving a hint of scent in their wake. Five, six. A long pause, and a total of twelve people had boarded.

She kept her eyes closed, listening to the door close, the driver engaging the transmission, and the hiss of the brakes. The bus lurched forward with some drivers, but not this one—Roger, she thought his name was—pulled away so smoothly, it was almost as if the bus wasn't moving at all.

Something brushed against her knees, then her right arm, and she opened her eyes. Startled, she saw Florence next to her. They'd never met away from Vivien's home. The ghost turned to her and smiled. Vivien feared she would want to talk.

She stared through the windshield, watching the road move under them. Gradually, fear gripped her. Not of Florence. She never felt afraid with Florence. Her fear rose because of another presence. Something behind, watching. The seat backs stood too high for her to turn around to look.

Roger pulled over at the store before Vivien pulled the bell cord. She got up and looked toward the back of the bus, seeing the faces of strangers looking elsewhere. Did a figure lurk in the deep shadows in the very back seats? Maybe. No.

She said thanks to Roger and climbed down. Florence walked silently beside her, disappearing only when they reached home. The hinges of the gate in the chain link fence squealed when she pushed it open and then closed it.

Dinner had just been set on the table. The games had started later and had lasted longer, making her late. She went into her bedroom and took off the sun dress to hang it in the bathroom on the shower curtain rod to air out.

Wearing shorts and a halter top felt so much more comfortable. She took a deep breath, then went to the table and sat down.

Her family spoke little, as usual, while they ate. At the end of the meal, Mama asked how it went at the tournament.

"No one threw a chess piece at anyone today," Vivien said. "They were pretty intense, though. They really take this game seriously."

There wasn't much else to tell. The only differences between yesterday and today were the fewer players and Florence's appearing on the bus. Not to mention the feeling of another presence. She couldn't tell them about that.

The girls finished cleaning the kitchen, and Vivien sat at the table and found her place in *The Martian Chronicles* by Ray Bradbury. He transported her to the colonies on the red planet until she looked out the window at the dry yard and lengthening shadows. The biggest differences between the fictional landscape and what she saw were slight.

The sun was setting when she put the book down and went outside. The deep red sky over the western horizon lightened to pink overhead. The sparse clouds to the east echoed the pink. The sun glowed yellow just above the horizon.

Vivien climbed onto the picnic table and listened to the music of the summer replacement variety show emanating from the open windows and door. She lay down, staring at the darkening sky. Soon, stars twinkled here and there.

"Are you all right?"

Vivien recognized the voice as Florence's. "I'm fine." She continued staring straight up.

The table vibrated slightly as the ghost sat on the bench. Vivien still marveled at the way ghosts could appear as living people—to her, at least. They could touch, they had weight, although they were no more than a puff of wind. Then she remembered seeing Wilbur speaking to Jakob, who didn't seem to detect his grandfather's presence.

"You saw him?" Florence asked.

"I saw someone. I'm guessing it was Wilbur Foxe. Is he the figure in the shadows on the stage?"

"Yes," Florence said so softly Vivien almost didn't hear.

"Can't you talk to him?"

"No."

"Why not?"

"He will not let me get near him."

"Is he afraid of you?" If the two ghosts can appear in the same place at the same time, why couldn't Florence make her own arrangements with Wilbur?

"It's almost as if we are on a different level."

"Did you come home with me because you were afraid he might hurt me?"

"I can get near you, but he can't. Well, I don't think he can. But he is watching you."

"Why?"

"I don't know."

"It has to be because of your wanting to play that final game."

"I don't know."

Silence fell between them. Vivien watched a falling star streak across the sky. She'd mentioned them to Daddy and he told her they were meteorites falling to Earth from space. They burned up as they passed through Earth's atmosphere. Where did he learn that?

She'd decided they might be ghosts coming back to torment people. Well, not torment. Maybe only to resolve the problems they left behind.

"Florence," she said, "would you be willing to play the game against Wilbur's son or grandson?"

"I want to play against Wilbur."

"We might not be able to convince him to do that."

"Jakob is not as good a player."

"He may be the only one we can convince." Vivien studied Florence's profile while she considered the possibility.

Florence nodded. "If that is all we can do, yes, I will play Jakob."

CHAPTER
SIXTEEN

The four remaining contestants took their seats. A small crowd had gathered, and they sat in chairs set apart, this time in rows near the tables. The players who were to move first with the white pieces were chosen, cigarettes were lit, glasses filled, and silence fell.

Instead of standing to one side in order to be visible to the players, Vivien and Jack had seats near the refreshment tables. The two judges sat on the other side of the players, close enough to see the play on both chess boards. Steven Lewis sat opposite Larry Pence. Vivien concentrated on Jakob Foxe, playing against Michael James, hoping to catch a glimpse of his grandfather's ghost. She felt certain he would show up today with the championship within reach.

From the stage, Mrs. Stirling rang the bell and announced, "Begin." Lewis and Jakob, each playing white, moved pawns forward. The play was slow, thoughtful. Twice, Vivien realized she held her breath.

Some in the audience whispered to each other. "He's using the Halloween Gambit," one man said. "His queen is in danger," from another. Many whispers she couldn't hear clearly. She wouldn't understand their comments if she did hear them. Pieces were captured and removed. After an hour, the players called for a break. Mrs. Stirling said, "Ten minutes."

**Everyone rose, stretching amid some groans. Glasses were refilled, either water, iced tea, or soda. Both players and watchers visited the bathrooms. A few went outside to smoke, hoping for a breeze, perhaps. Fans were readjusted to improve air flow. Vivien expected the contestants to return quickly, but they re-entered the auditorium slowly and resumed their seats.

Jakob took a long drink from his glass, which Vivien had refilled. He seemed nervous. She wondered if he'd been expecting Wilbur to be there to help. So far, there'd been no sign of his grandfather, and she guessed he might be in danger of losing. She looked toward the stage. No shadowy figure lurked at the back. Had he decided not to help his grandson today?

If Wilbur had helped before, why wouldn't he help now? That assumed, of course, that Jakob knew his grandfather's ghost had been there or heard him whispering in his ear, a form of cheating no one could prove.

Play resumed and several pieces were moved. Jakob paused longer between moves. Vivien guessed he was in trouble. Suddenly Wilbur, appeared, whispering in his grandson's ear. Jakob reached toward a piece, and his grandfather turned his head to smile at Vivien. Another hour passed. Jakob did win. Wilbur faded away, and James flipped his king over. The two men stood and shook hands. Jakob would play in the final game next day against Mr. Lewis. When he walked away from the table, he also looked at Vivien. Could he know of her interest in his family?

GAME OF THE DEAD

∽

With only two games left, Vivien climbed aboard the bus an hour earlier than the day before. Excitement about the next day's play filled her mind with scenes of triumph and loss, blocking the images of Jakob and Wilbur gloating. In the beginning, her favorites were the two girls, and seeing one of them reach the fourth level justified her belief in them. Still, it was best for her purposes that Jakob win the tournament.

She hoped Jakob's winning would make Wilbur welcome the challenge of playing against Florence but she needed to speak to him. What she didn't know was how to get him to come to her.

After dinner and after the sun had set, Vivien went out to her usual spot on the picnic table. The crescent moon floated in the darkness. June was half over. Two more months of summer vacation and heat and no rain. A soft wind blew across her, drying the sweat on her skin. Instead of thinking about chess and tournaments, her thoughts turned to the start of school and books and studying, which seemed so far away. In the middle of summer, she wished for cooler weather.

"Why do you pursue me?" a man's voice asked.

She sat up quickly and swung her legs off the table. She planted her feet firmly on the bench in case she had to jump to the ground. Whoever the man was, he wasn't showing himself.

"Wilbur?"

He materialized slightly to her right. His face shone pale in the darkness. She relaxed, not wanting him to think she was afraid.

"I haven't pursued you. I did see you helping your grandson cheat. Too bad he isn't as good a player as you were."

He was silent a moment, then said, "It is. I'm still as good as ever. Better than any of those in your tournament."

Vivien started to say it wasn't her tournament, but she couldn't let him bait her with trivialities. "Yet, Jakob needed your help."

"Mr. Jakob Foxe to you."

"He barely won today."

"You know nothing about chess."

"Because I'm a girl?"

"Of course."

He moved two steps closer and Vivien tensed.

"No woman or girl ever beat me. Few men have ever beat me."

"You never played Florence Macartan did you? Did you kill her?"

"Heavens to Betsy, no. I felt no need to go that far."

"Someone did."

"Why would you think that? Just because someone buried her in the woods, far from town?"

How did he know where she was buried if he wasn't the one who put her there? "She played well enough for someone to be afraid of her."

"I assume you and she intend to goad me into playing against her." He chuckled as if he thought the idea ridiculous.

"Why would we?" She stretched her legs out one at a time. "She thinks you owe her that final game, of course. And she'd love to prove to herself whether or not she could beat you. Then, you have nothing to prove, do you? Except you'll never know for sure."

"Yes, I do."

With that, he faded away. He'd sounded angry through the entire conversation, and Vivien couldn't be certain he would play against Florence. Where was she, anyway? Did she know Wilbur had come?

He'll play Florence. If he doesn't, Jakob might be goaded into it.

If we can do that, Wilbur will have to step in. Wilbur was the stronger player, and neither of them wanted to lose to a female.

The theme music for *Wanted: Dead or Alive* wafted through the open door of the trailer, and she slid off the table. She hadn't decided if the star, Steve McQueen, was a heartthrob yet, but she never missed watching the show.

She went to bed early since she had been getting up earlier the past few mornings and wanted to be fresh tomorrow. The last game should be very exciting. For a chess match, that is. She chose not to speculate on whether Florence didn't appear tonight because of Wilbur Foxe's presence. She didn't come every night, anyway.

She dreamed of large chess pieces walking around and bumping into each other. They fell and rolled around on the floor, kicking their little legs, trying to get up.

CHAPTER
SEVENTEEN

Mrs. Stirling had been right when predicting a large crowd would show up for the final game. At least twenty-five people milled around the room, talking, most holding a cold drink in one hand and waving a cigarette in the other. Cigars had been forbidden since women were present, and their fumes in a somewhat confined space would have been unbearable for everyone.

After the three days already passed, Mrs. Stirling decided it would be best to leave the doors open for better ventilation. With two fans blowing toward the doors, it made a big difference in the amount of smoke hanging in the air.

A single table sat in place, the board set up, and the strain of expectation pressed against everyone. Jakob Foxe stood a little apart from the crowd, while Steven Lewis stood in the midst of a group of well-wishers.

Vivien stood behind the refreshment table as usual. She fingered the amulet on a chain around her neck. It had been given to her by Hester, Mignon's grandmother who was Roma. Mignon, died several years earlier at the same age Vivien was when they met. Mignon became her best friend who wanted Vivien to stay with her forever, which would have required Vivien's death. Regret for realizing her friend's desires still overwhelmed her at times.

After her encounter with Wilbur the night before, Vivien dug out the pendant. She hadn't worn it since leaving France a year earlier because it was to be worn for protection from hants or ghosts.

The bell rang, and from the stage, Mrs. Stirling asked the contestants to take their seats. Jakob stood behind his chair, waiting for his opponent to reach the table. Lewis smiled, joking with those around him, while they patted him on the back. He approached the opposite side of the table. He and Jakob shook hands, and they sat.

"A break will be called after the first hour," Mrs. Stirling announced. "Gentlemen, do either of you need a drink, an ash tray?"

Both men shook their heads no.

The onlookers all took seats, settling down to watch the two best players of the tournament go head-to-head.

"Then let's begin."

One of the two judges approached the table and held out his hands. In each he held a king, white in one hand and black in the other. He turned his back to switch the pieces from hand to hand several times. When he turned again, he held out his hands, gripping the pieces tightly so they couldn't be seen. Mr. Lewis, being the older player, chose the right hand, which revealed the white king.

"Mr. Lewis will play first," Mrs. Stirling announced. She reiterated the rules, the role of the judges, then rang the bell again. "Begin."

Mr. Lewis moved a pawn forward two squares. Jakob moved his opposite pawn forward so the two pieces faced each other. Play continued slowly, the players and audience intent on the board. After several moves, someone whispered, "He's using the King's Gambit." Another man nodded.

Play proceeded as before. The heat in the room felt more intense than any of the previous days, in spite of the open doors. Pieces were captured and removed from the board. The onlookers whispered.

Jakob looked up at the school clock mounted above the stage. They'd been playing fifty-eight minutes. He took his handkerchief from his pants pocket and wiped his forehead. Vivien realized he was in trouble. Would he stall until the hour ended? Where was his grandfather?

Mrs. Stirling called for the break. The contestants stood. Lewis stretched and rolled his shoulders. Both men moved away from the table as required. Jakob stood near the refreshment table, biting his knuckle. He seemed not to notice the people milling around.

Spectators talked of the heat accompanied by the clink of glasses being filled with ice for cold drinks. They were allowed no discussion of the game, of course.

Vivien glanced at the stage. In the shadows at the back, a figure moved slightly. Had Wilbur been watching from there the whole time? Jakob, standing off to one side, looked nervous until, suddenly, his grandfather stood beside him, whispering in his ear. She could almost see a lightbulb go on above his head. Just like in the comic books.

People shuffled in and out, visiting the restroom or smoking outside. They rushed back inside at the sound of the bell and resumed their seats. Quiet descended.

Wilbur appeared beside Jakob, who studied the board for only a moment before moving his knight to take Lewis's bishop. Play became even slower than in the first hour. Perspiration covered Jakob's forehead, which he wiped with his handkerchief frequently. Lewis appeared relaxed, in control. Either that or he didn't care as much about winning.

Suddenly, the game was over. Jakob had moved his queen to protect the king, placing her in the path of a lowly pawn, one of the few still on the board. Wilbur looked murderously at his grandson and watched Lewis move his bishop to checkmate. Jakob stared at the pieces. Reluctantly, he turned his king over.

Lewis smiled and stood, holding out his hand to Jakob, who rose slowly. He held out his own hand, and Lewis shook it vigorously.

"Good game, Jakob," Lewis said.

Jakob nodded. At the start of the game, he hadn't looked confident. Not until his grandfather appeared and whispered in his ear. Vivien had noticed that Jakob never looked toward his grandfather, and she'd concluded whatever he whispered to his grandson was taken as an inspiration of his own. Jakob never realized Wilbur stood beside him.

Wilbur looked at Vivien. She didn't waver, but the anger in his eyes made her afraid. He took a step toward her. He clearly wanted to make someone pay. She clutched the amulet, the coolness of the stones pressing against the palm of her hand. She held out her other hand to ward off the ghost.

"If Mr. Foxe and Mr. Lewis will come to the stage, we will present the trophies," Mrs. Stirling said.

Wilbur faded. Two men standing near the refreshment table looked at Vivien oddly, and she put her hand down. The room grew quiet. She smiled at the two men, and they took their seats in the audience.

Meanwhile, the two contestants had reached the stage, one standing to Mrs. Stirling's right, the other to her left. A man with a camera appeared, snapping pictures with a bright flash. Jakob received a small loving cup for second place. Mr. Lewis received a medium-sized trophy for first place. They expressed their thanks for everyone who made the tournament possible, to polite applause.

Vivien approached the stage as Jakob walked down the steps. "May I speak to you?" she asked. The cameraman interviewed the winner at the foot of the steps, writing in a notebook.

"Not now."

"I need to ask you —"

"This is neither the time nor the place."

"Where and when? Just tell me and I'll be there."

"We have nothing to discuss."

"You don't know what I want to ask you."

"Florence Macartan," Jakob said. "No woman, young or old, should expect to compete against men, particularly a Negro woman." He walked stiffly toward the door.

A Negro woman? Florence was a Negro? No, she would have noticed. Vivien focused on Jakob as he made his way through the crowd, accepting congratulations from several fellow chess players.

So, Jakob knew about Florence and that she, Vivien, knew about the game played decades earlier. Of course, he probably heard about the tournament of 1910 from his father, maybe even his grandfather. Would Wilbur have told hi anything at all about Vivien?

But Florence. She couldn't be a Negro. Every article published against her participation, every word would have condemned her.

Eventually, the room cleared except for those cleaning everything up. Furniture was put away, dishes were washed, and food and drinks packed away for Mrs. Stirling to take home. She gave both Jack and Vivien a cold soda to drink on the way home.

"Thank you both for your hard work. I will be sending a letter to your school to let them know how valuable your assistance was." She climbed into her car, and they stood on the sidewalk, watching her drive away.

"It's been fun working with you," Jack said to Vivien.

She felt herself blush, unsure why. "I had fun, too. Maybe we'll see each other around school."

"Probably. Especially now I know who you are." He took a sip of the root beer and turned to leave.

For the first time, she realized he didn't have a car, or at least he hadn't driven it today. Most of the older kids in high school had some sort of vehicle, the boys preferring pickup trucks. She shrugged and started walking to the bus station, all the while wondering about how Jakob knew about her. Or what he knew, for that matter.

More than that, she tried to come to terms with the possibility Florence was a Negro. Why did she never say?

CHAPTER
EIGHTEEN

The stars sparkled as usual in the black sky. The day's heat hadn't let up in spite of the sun's setting. Vivien lay on top of the picnic table, trying to think about what she'd learned from Jakob. It boiled down to Jakob knowing more than she thought. Perhaps he did hear his grandfather's ghost, and Florence was a Negro. How could she not know?

Where was she? She needed to talk to her. She heard a rustle near the table.

"Florence?"

"I am here, Vivien."

"Why didn't you tell me?" Vivien sat up and swung her legs off the table, resting her feet on the bench where the ghost sat.

"I didn't know how you'd feel about helping me if you knew. Most of the time, I have come to you in the dark, which made it difficult for you to see. My mother was white, and my skin was very light."

"You had to know that if I helped you, I would find out."

"By then it would be too late if I were lucky. Hopefully, you would have arranged everything, and I would play chess against Mr. Foxe."

"It doesn't make much difference to me, but if I'd known I could have —" What could—or would—she have done differently? "Does your being buried where you were have anything to do with your race?"

"Yes."

Vivien waited for Florence to explain. Meanwhile, she imagined all sorts of reasons which would not have occurred to her before.

"You know that in much of the United States it is illegal for two people of different races to marry," Florence said.

Vivien had never heard that. She stayed quiet, letting Florence continue.

"Lorenz, Mr. Foxe's son, and I were in love. He was a year older than me. His father did not know, and we didn't know how to be together without getting arrested. Mr. Foxe would have been very unhappy if he found out, and we were very careful not to give him any reason to think about it."

She described the end of the semi-final game and that she knew Lorenz, who watched every game, rooted for her to win. She did win, as did Mr. Foxe. Lorenz winked at her and she left the school quickly but with a warm feeling in her heart. She tried to forget the animosity toward her, which had been so thick in the air she felt like she was choking at times. She had enough to worry about with the final game to be played the next day.

She went to high school and signed up for the tournament using her mother's maiden name.

"In those days, Killeen was a whites only town and proud of it. The city council had advertised for an experienced plumber to lead in extending a water system that would serve more homes. Papa sent a letter applying; they responded with questions. A few more letters back and forth and he was offered the job."

They hadn't known about the racial makeup of the town until they arrived by train. In spite of the shock at Mr. Grooms being Negro, the city council decided to pay him to do the work. He'd produced glowing letters of recommendation, and they needed someone who could do a good job. Her father bought a piece of land on the edge of town and a small house for his wife and five children. Florence was the youngest and somewhat spoiled, she admitted.

They believed he and his family would move on once the work was finished.

"Mama kept out of sight as much as possible. Marcus, the eldest, did the shopping and any chores requiring going into town. The house was isolated enough that no one else saw my family and no one would ever come for a visit."

"You speak so well," Vivien said. "Did they let you go to school in Killeen?" She was realizing she didn't know much about how Negros were treated fifty years ago. She also didn't know much about how they were treated in her own time. Surely, it was better. For instance, kids of all races attended schools in Killeen, just as they had in Fontenet.

Florence shook her head. "Mama taught us at home until we moved here. She was the daughter of an important white man, and he sent her to a finishing school in Virginia. She was so smart. She taught me to play chess. By the time I was ten I beat her every time. She said I took to it like a duck to water."

Florence took Vivien's hands in hers. "That night I hurried home to tell Mama I'd won."

Vivien felt how much she'd wanted to get home where she would be safe. Florence's fear took Vivien's breath away. When a car's lights lit up the road ahead of her, she became even more afraid. The car stopped, and she left the road, running toward the woods not far from the road, hoping to hide in the darkness beyond the light.

"No, you don't," a man's voice said behind her. Arms wrapped around her and picked her up. "You're coming with me." She recognized Wilbur Foxe's voice.

She kicked and screamed while he carried her to the car. He put a hand over her mouth and she tried to bite him. He threw her face down into the back seat of his new Model T Ford, of which he was so proud. He put his knee in her back to hold her down while he tied her hands and feet together.

"Papa?"

"Be quiet, Lorenz."

Lorenz? She wanted to shout to him to help her, but Mr. Foxe tied his handkerchief around her mouth. She called Lorenz's name, but it came out muffled.

"Papa, what are you going to do?"

"We're going to teach this little upstart a lesson."

They drove for quite a while. When they finally stopped and Wilbur pulled her out of the car, they stood on a dirt road next to a growth of trees and underbrush. He picked her up and threw her over his shoulder. Brambles and branches tore at her as he made his way deep into the thicket.

Finally, he stopped and dumped her to the ground. Tears blurred her vision, but she saw both Mr. Foxe and Lorenz a short distance from her. They argued, and in a rage, Mr. Foxe hit Lorenz, knocking him to the ground.

"You don't have to help me, but you sure ain't gonna stop me," Mr. Foxe said.

She pushed with her feet, trying to scoot backward. Vines and branches caught at her. He knelt beside her and grabbed her hair to lift her head off the ground.

"This ends it," he said. "Bad enough you're a woman child, but I won't lose to a darkie."

He held up a knife, and she tried to kick him. "Please," she screamed, but the gag turned it into a whisper.

He punched her in the stomach with the knife. At first she only felt the pain of not being able to breathe. A greater pain followed, burning along nerves, reaching her brain. She gulped for air, trying to reach beyond the pain.

Vivien panted, trying to get enough air. She hadn't simply watched what happened. It happened to her. Being thrown to the ground. Wilbur's gripping her hair. What felt like a punch in the stomach.

She trembled with pain and anger. He had no right to treat Florence that way, regardless of her skin color or her gender. She brushed tears from her cheeks.

"He killed you?" she whispered.

Florence nodded. "Everything went black. I don't know how long. I sort of came to later. The sky had turned pale and birds sang all around me. I looked down and saw myself—my body—lying in a tangle of vines and brambles. My eyes were open. I didn't understand, and I was so afraid. I heard someone coming, making lots of noise as he fought his way toward me. I wanted to run away but I couldn't move."

Lorenz appeared, carrying a shovel and a large tarp slung over his shoulder. He knelt beside Florence's body and brushed a strand of hair from her forehead. She moved to him, wanting to let him know she was there, but she couldn't touch him. She spoke, but he didn't hear her. She looked around for Wilbur, but he wasn't in sight.

He wrapped her in the tarp as gently as possible, blocking her view, and she heard him clear away the brush so he could dig a hole with a long-handled shovel. When it was large enough, he lay her in it, tucking the tarp around her, and shoveled the dirt over her.

Vivien saw it with her own eyes, but somehow she felt it,

too. When the grave was covered, he walked around, using the shovel to push vegetation out of his way. He moved out of sight, returning a moment later, carrying a squarish piece of wood. He sat down with it and carved Florence's name with a pocketknife. When it was done, he placed it at the head of the grave in a shallow trench and packed dirt around it. He stood straight and wiped away tears with dirty hands.

The sky had turned to bright blue, and he knelt beside the grave, his hands pressed together as if in prayer. "I'm so sorry, Flo. If I'd know what he meant to do . . ."

CHAPTER
NINETEEN

The scene faded. "How could he?" Vivien straightened her shoulders, trying to sit up straight.

"He loved me."

"But he —"

"He loved Wilbur so much," Florence said. "He respected him and believed in him."

"You're making excuses for him because you still love him."

"Can a ghost love someone? I wonder."

"Is there any way to prove what Wilbur did?"

"I don't care about that. I only want to play one game against him."

"Well, he can't threaten you anymore," Vivien said.

"No, but he can threaten you. I'm sorry I got you involved."

"Not to mention his grandson knows me." Did he know her name or where she lived?

There wasn't much more to say for the moment. Florence apologized again for perhaps putting her in danger and disappeared.

Inside, *Seahunt* was on TV, and Vivien dropped into the

empty chair next to the sofa. Haunted by what she'd seen and heard, she went to bed before the show ended. She lay in bed and heard Mama tell Daddy, "She's tired. She worked pretty hard at that tournament and walking in that heat." Daddy mumbled something. Vivien suspected Mama had convinced him coming and going on her own was a necessary part of growing up, especially for her. Mama always called her too independent for her own good, and Daddy often squelched her independence.

Vivien still lay awake when Lauren complained about having to go to bed. She tromped into the bathroom, making the trailer rattle. Water ran as she washed up, and she went to her to her bed with less drama. The end of an ordinary Sunday night.

∼

Vivien spent the first part of the week following the tournament, trying to think of some way to contact either Jakob or Lorenz. She believed the only way to get Wilbur to play against Florence was through them. With the tournament over, she had lost the most direct avenue.

Wednesday night, she sat in the dark at the picnic table, as always. She loved watching the stars and had come to recognize their movement across the sky. Mama had suggested she should stay with the family watching TV or maybe read in her bedroom. "I worry sometimes about your need to be alone."

"I can think better," Vivien said. After a moment, she asked, "Do you know why we see ghosts and become involved in their troubles?" They were sitting at the dining table drinking iced tea while Lauren and Daddy sat in the living room with the TV on.

"No one knows the reason. At least I've never heard, and your grandma hasn't either."

Vivien hesitated to go on. Hester had told her the reason the last time she visited the Roma camp on the hill behind her house. At least, she hoped it wasn't just a tale the old woman made up. Hester had both hindered and helped her with Mignon's ghost. Working against her granddaughter hadn't been easy. The last time Vivien saw the woman, she told what she'd seen of Vivien's family. She remembered what she said, word for word.

Vivien felt the need to tell Mama the whole story but did she want to know? Vivien took a deep breath and repeated the words.

"Your first ancestor to set foot in America had a son. Born there. As a young man, he fell in love with a young woman indentured to his family. He promised to marry her, but his parents judged the girl to be unsuitable. They found another girl from a wealthy family, and he married her.

"The woman he loved objected, and his family had her charged with some offense. She was flogged and lost the baby. Their son's baby. She never recovered from the beating, and on her deathbed she cursed the son's wife and daughters she would bear. His wife lost her mind after giving birth to two daughters. She screamed about seeing ghosts hovering over her as they were born."

Mama .ed to the story and smiled. "How could the Gypsy woman know about our family?"

"Roma," Vivien corrected without thinking. "She knew many things. I wish I could have stayed so she could teach me." Vivien made overlapping wet circles on the table with the glass. "So, do you think that's a good reason generations of women in our family see ghosts?"

Mama shrugged. "It's as good an explanation as any other."

Did Mama believe the old woman's explanation or not? It certainly didn't put their ancestors in a good light. And why should they pay for something that happened more than a century earlier?

At the picnic table, Vivien sat thinking of the story as the woman related it in heavily accented English. She missed many things about France, and her voice was one of them. Mignon's voice came to her then, her laugh, and how she adored clothes. At times, she regretted not staying with her, but only for a moment.

The gate opened with a grating noise. Vivien stiffened. Someone moved around the front of the trailer trying not to make any noise.

She slid off the table and started toward the trailer. She opened her mouth to shout, "Daddy!"

Strong arms went around her from behind, pinning her arms to her sides. One hand reached up and clamped over her mouth. She struggled to free herself, as Florence had struggled against Wilbur Foxe.

The man dragged her through the gate and down the dirt road to the next trailer. The door stood open, and he lifted her inside. He shoved her onto the sofa, face down, pinning her with his knee, then he pulled her hands behind her and tied them together. He moved off her and stood panting beside the sofa. She gagged at the smell of too much aftershave mixed with sweat.

CHAPTER
TWENTY

Vivien turned her head to the side so she could catch her breath. Dust and mold in the cushion made her cough. The man stood near, darker than the surrounding darkness. For the second time, she was bound and helpless, only this time was for real.

"Well now, missy, you're in a fix aren't you?"

The wife beater and former neighbor breathed hard, and his voice sounded triumphant.

"I guess you never did find your wife," she said, unable to keep from goading him.

He slapped the back of her head. "Don't talk."

"Now you've got me, what are you going to do?"

"Nothing you'll like." He chuckled. "I'm going to enjoy this."

She felt the trailer vibrate as if someone had stepped inside. Her captor didn't seem to notice since he was too busy pacing and describing what he planned to do to her. She didn't quite hear what he said because of a ringing in her ears.

Then came a cracking noise. Her captor grunted and

slumped to the floor face first. She couldn't turn her head far enough to see who hit him. Fingers worked at the binding on her hands, and finally they came loose.

Her arms and legs were weak and turning over was difficult. "Who are you?" she managed to say once she sat upright. A dark figure leaned over the prone one. He worked at tying her attacker's hands with the rope used to tie hers.

The figure stood, and she heard the "clink" of a Zippo lighter being opened, then the "scritch" of lighting it. The man held the lighter so that he could see her face, illuminating his own at the same time. It was Lorenz Foxe.

"Mr. Foxe. What are you doing here?"

"I came to talk to you. I turned the corner at the end of your road and saw that man carrying you through the gate and into here. Who is he?"

"He used to live here. He beat his wife, and I helped her get away. I thought he'd left for good."

"Apparently not."

She agreed. It surprised her when he didn't question her actions or ask why she thought she had the right to interfere in someone's marriage.

"He either wanted to punish me or find out where she went. I don't know where she went." Dizziness overwhelmed her, and she leaned over to put her head between her knees, like she'd seen a teacher instruct a girl to do in class.

"What did you want to talk to me about?" she asked when the dizziness passed.

"Florence Macartan. How do you know about her?"

Mama's voice calling her name caught their attention.

"I have to go or she'll come looking for me. I don't want her to know about this."

"Can we meet somewhere?"

Vivien thought only a moment. "The library on Friday at eleven."

She stood and left the trailer while she made up a story about the man tied up on the floor. She'd have to find an excuse to go to the library an extra day.

"Where've you been?" Mama asked.

"I thought I heard something in the trailer next door," she said. "I went to see but I was too afraid to go inside. I'd just started back here when you called."

"Glenn, there may be more trouble next door."

Daddy got up from the sofa. "Why?"

"Vivien heard something over there."

"I'll check." He got a flashlight from the kitchen drawer and left.

Vivien hoped Lorenz had enough time to get to his car down the road, just this side of the streetlight. She stepped outside to look. It was gone. For a moment, she worried that the former neighbor might tell what happened and she'd be in trouble, at least with Mama and Daddy. She reasoned that would mean also telling that he'd kidnapped her. Police questioning him might be able to get him to tell the truth, like they did on TV. Nothing she could do about it now.

Daddy went into the neighbor's trailer and the lights came on. Another moment and he stepped back out. He hurried to the fence, and Mama got half-way across to it.

"Call the police," he said. "The bastard's back, but someone tied him up." He went back into the trailer, and Vivien followed Mama inside.

A Killeen Police Department patrol car pulled up twelve minutes later, lights flashing and dust rising as it skidded to a stop in the gravel driveway. The officer got out and walked to the door of the trailer. It looked like he had his hand on the gun at his waist. Mama went to the fence. Vivien didn't follow. She didn't want to see the man who twice tried to hurt her, nor did she want him to see her.

Neighbors, attracted by the flashing lights on the patrol car, stood along the road. Most of them had probably been watching TV until finding this real-life drama more interesting. After forty-five minutes or so, the policeman brought the man outside. He was handcuffed. The officer put him in the back seat and drove away. The lights had gone out inside, and Daddy stepped out.

Vivien sat on the couch next to Lauren and waited. When he came in, Daddy put his hand on Mama's arm, reassuring her. Lauren gave him her seat on the sofa, and she and Mama sat in the chairs.

"It was Arnold," he said while sitting next to Vivien. "Why he came back, I don't know. He said someone came up from behind and hit him. He woke up just before we untied him. I told the officer about his threatening Vivien." He reached over and patted her hand. "And why. I don't know if I convinced the officer I wasn't the one who hit him."

"He couldn't blame you if you did," Mama said.

"We'll see." He exhaled deeply.

"Why did the policeman arrest him?" Mama asked.

"Trespassing for now. I told the officer he might be AWOL—absent without leave. They're going to check. If he is, they'll hand him over to the Army. Anyway, that's enough excitement. Let's get to bed."

It was late, and Vivien was exhausted. However, she lay on the bed, unable to sleep. She threw back the sheet trying to get cooler. The heat wasn't the only thing keeping her awake, of course. Both the attack on her and Lorenz Foxe saving her kept running through her mind.

It was so like Florence's struggle against Wilbur Foxe, except Florence died. She might have died, too. She didn't thank Lorenz. If only he'd been able to save Florence, too, all those years ago.

∾

Friday came, and Lauren decided not to go to the library because Sylvia and her family were going to Lake Belton to swim and they invited her to go with them. That made it easier for Vivien to meet Lorenz Foxe without having to answer a bunch of questions.

Vivien watched her sister skipping down the dusty road, waving to her friend. Although Lauren always made friends easily, there had always been a bond between the two of them, especially when the only kids they knew were each other. She gulped at the sense of loss that washed through her and walked in the opposite direction to catch the bus.

The heat hadn't let up, and she was sweating by the time she entered the library. The cool air wrapped around her, and she shivered. She spoke to the librarian at the circulation desk and slid the books she was returning into the slot. The table she always used was unoccupied. She set her bag on top and went looking for Lorenz in case he'd arrived first.

She didn't see him anywhere, so she went into the fiction stacks. She wasn't in the mood for science fiction this time. She'd been thinking of the Alexandre Dumas book and decided she wanted to read more. She returned to the table with several books and spotted Lorenz coming down another aisle. She moved toward him until he spotted her.

"Over here," she called and led the way to her table. He set a box on the table, the picture on the top a chessboard set up to play.

"I thought this would make a good excuse for us to sit together. I'll teach you a bit about the game."

"Sure," she said. "I'll help set out the pieces. I know that much. Well, mostly."

Her only mistake was getting the white king and queen on the wrong squares. When he told her, she switched them. He handed her a small paperback book on beginner chess with a bookmark. "Turn to the page I've marked."

Lorenz had given her the white pieces, so she moved first, following the moves shown in the book. "If we have time, we can play that game through, and you can get an idea of what each play means."

"Thanks, but I'd rather talk about Florence," Vivien said.

"I know. But we need to have the game further along, so it looks like we're playing."

They moved pieces for the next ten minutes, and she began to understand how the king could be threatened. He started to move his bishop to the right of the king but didn't quite touch the piece.

"I was in love with Florence," he said softly. He put his hand flat on the table beside the board.

"I know."

"How?"

"She told me."

"What are you, some sort of Gypsy or fortune teller?"

Vivien couldn't possibly tell him she saw the murder in the woods. Nor about seeing him return to bury her. She looked down at the board. Neither spoke for several minutes.

"I acted like a coward," he said. "No, I *was* a coward, and didn't protect her as I should have."

"She has . . . I've heard her voice. At first, I didn't understand what she wanted. She wants me to persuade your father to play the last game against her."

"How? He's dead." Lorenz leaned away from the table. "I don't understand."

With the exception of Mignon, whose grandmother may or may not have seen her, no one else had ever seen or heard the ghosts she'd encountered, except Lauren. She lifted her head and met Lorenz's gaze.

"This isn't your first encounter, is it?" he asked.

"No. I've helped a few others and I intend to do what I can to help Florence get what she wants."

"Does that include proving my father killed her?"

"No. She only wants to play the game."

"How can I help?" He reached down and moved the bishop. "Check."

～

DADDY CAME HOME EARLY that afternoon. The police contacted him on post and said they wanted to question Vivien.

"They still think I might have attacked Arnold because of what he tried to do to Vivien before. They're waiting for me to take you in to the station."

Dizziness made her sway, and Mama led her to the sofa. The fear of being interrogated by policemen didn't last. They only wanted her to confirm that she heard Arnold in the trailer and her father went over after she reported what she heard.

Don't say too much.

She repeated the words over and over while Daddy drove her to the station. Mama had asked if she wanted her to go along. Vivien said no, Daddy would be there.

A woman police officer guided her into a bare room with a table and several chairs. Daddy couldn't go with her. She'd seen enough police interrogations on TV to not be surprised. When she became aware she was twisting the handkerchief she brought over and over, she stuck it in the pocket of her shorts.

The woman officer stood in the corner, and soon a male detective came in. "I'm Detective Barth," he said.

"Hello."

"I just need to ask a couple of questions about what happened the other night. You were outside of your trailer?"

"Yes."

"Why were you outside so late?"

"I like to look at the stars."

"You were alone?"

"Yes."

"No boyfriend. Or girlfriend?"

"No." She felt like giggling.

"And you heard something in the trailer next door."

She nodded.

"What sort of noise was it?"

She shrugged. "Just a noise."

"Did it sound like two people struggling? Or voices?"

"It was sort of muffled."

"You went over to check it out."

"Yes."

"That could have been dangerous."

She was getting tired of his voice, the condescending tone, as if she wasn't a mature fifteen. "I heard the noise, I went over but didn't open the door. I got scared because of what happened before, and I didn't know if Arnold had come back. I ran home and told Mama. Daddy went over to check. We called the police."

She had leaned forward, putting her elbows on the table, as she recounted what happened. Now, she leaned back and folded her hands in her lap.

The detective glanced at the woman officer, and a vague smile passed between them. "Very good," he said. "I think that's all we need."

"I can go?"

"Yes. And I don't think you need to be afraid of Mr. Arnold anymore. Thank you for coming in."

The woman led her to the entrance where Daddy waited. He hugged her and looked at the detective.

"We're done."

Daddy nodded, and they got in the car.

"They didn't really think you tied up Mr. Arnold, did they?" she asked. It was a little past dinner time and her stomach growled.

"No, I don't think so. They wanted to tie up all the loose ends."

"Good."

"We won't have to worry about Mr. Arnold again," Daddy said. "He is AWOL and the Army will be locking him up a while."

Vivien started to say she knew what AWOL meant but decided it didn't matter.

Lauren was excited when they got home and wanted Vivien to relate all the details of what happened. Her sister would have to wait until after dinner. Going out to the picnic table when it got dark didn't seem like a good idea. Instead, Vivien stayed up and watched TV with her family.

CHAPTER
TWENTY-ONE

Monday was the Fourth of July. Plans were made to visit a display of armored vehicles on post. The Army cooks set up tables of food, but it was too hot to stay and eat outside. Vivien and her family piled paper plates high with sliced roast beef, burgers, and buns with all the fixings, then wrapped them with foil and took them home to eat later.

They stayed inside, trying to keep cool with sweet iced tea, the water cooler, and a couple of electric fans. Daddy didn't even putter around with the car, which he almost always did when nothing else was going on. He wasn't a reader, so he kept busy polishing brass and boots.

Vivien and Lauren read and moved around as little as possible. They ate at the usual time, stuffing themselves just as they would have at the cookout, except Mama insisted they eat off of her good plastic plates instead of the paper ones. After dark, they sat outside in the lawn chairs and watched fireworks visible over Killeen and listened to a holiday special on TV playing patriotic music. They were several miles away and couldn't hear the boom of the explosions, however the music made a great background.

It was later than usual when the girls went to bed. Vivien still lay awake when Mama and Daddy went to bed later, finding it impossible to sleep in the heat and with so much on her mind. Daddy started snoring, adding to the things keeping her awake. She got out of bed and stood in front of the water cooler in the dining room window, what some called a swamp cooler, even though the air blown on her was hardly cool.

She sneaked out to the picnic table, hoping to catch a breeze. Tonight, she found the wooden table almost too hard to lie on. She'd tried a pillow once, but it raised her head too high to see the stars straight overhead. Maybe spreading a blanket over the top would help with the hardness, but most of those they had were wool army blankets and very scratchy.

She lay spread eagle, exposing as much of her skin to the slight breeze as she could. A falling star streaked across the suffocatingly black sky, almost too fast to see.

She wiped her arms with her hands, feeling the sweat on her skin. She hated the heat and believed she would leave Texas once she graduated from high school. That would mean leaving her family, too. She wasn't sure she could do that.

She heard a soft noise next to the table, and thoughts of moving away vanished. Florence stood close and Vivien sat up, crossing her legs Indian-style, then uncrossed them because the skin of her legs stuck together. She scooted to the edge of the table and rested her feet on the bench.

"You met with Lorenz? How is he?"

"Don't you know?"

The ghost nodded. "He seemed sad to me."

"I guess he's been sad every day since you died."

"Surely there has been happiness in his life. His wife and son."

"Probably. But he still loves you. Or the memory of you."

"What do you mean?" Florence sat at the end of the bench.

"He's in love with who you were all those years ago. If you were still together, you would both be different, as much as he is different now."

"Yes, I imagine so."

"Anyway," Vivien said, changing the subject, "he and I are meeting at the library again Wednesday. We're hoping Wilbur might be persuaded to meet with us."

"Do you believe you can convince him?"

"I don't know. He killed you rather than take a chance on losing to you in the tournament. The best way might be telling him he would never have beaten you. He was afraid of you."

"I was never afraid of losing to her," Wilbur's voice cut in. "If you think that, you little guttersnipe, you have an exaggerated belief in your own skill."

He stood at the end of the table to Vivien's left and both drew away.

"Why did you kill her, then?" Vivien asked.

"Because of Lorenz," Wilbur said. "She wasn't suitable for him."

"That was up to him," Vivien said.

Florence touched Vivien's knee and nodded.

"We aren't interested in that," Vivien said. "We want to know if you're man enough to answer Florence's challenge and play a final game against her."

"I do not have anything to prove," he said, his voice spiteful. "Not to you, not to Lorenz."

"Yet, Jakob lost his game in spite of your helping him," Vivien reminded him.

"He stopped listening to me. Made his own mistake. If he'd listened to me —"

"The game might have ended sooner," Vivien said.

"Of course not!"

"Well, we just thought if you played a game against Florence now, you might finally find peace," Vivien said.

"I am at peace."

"Not here, you aren't."

Florence finally spoke. "I saw the fear in your eyes when you realized I would be your opponent in the final game for the championship. As did Lorenz. Your own son believes you are a coward."

"He knows nothing —"

"Maybe Jakob could be convinced to play against me," Florence said. "He needs to re-establish his claim to being strong and a great chess player to please his grandfather."

"I forbid it!"

"He's a grown man and can make the decision himself. Vivien can contact him and see if it can be arranged. Of course, she will tell him you refused to play."

"You think he will believe a ghost wants to beat him in a game of chess?"

"Perhaps if Florence shows him what she showed me," Vivien said.

"He won't go against me. He's adored me since he was a child. Believed what I told him. He won't believe you."

Perhaps it was Wilbur's influence over his grandson that enabled Jakob to hear his grandfather's instructions during the game. If so, could he also hear Florence? Could he see either of them?

"Does he know anything about Florence?" Vivien asked.

"No, why would he?"

"I think he should."

Florence looked from one to the other as they spoke.

"He won't believe —"

"Maybe not," Vivien interrupted him, "but he will begin to

wonder. I'm sure he understands that you are fanatical about being good at the game, that you'd do almost anything to win."

"I won't let you."

"How can you stop me?" Vivien asked. He'd disappeared. Probably just as well since she didn't really want to know what he might do. She turned to Florence. "You don't think he'd harm Jakob, do you? His own grandson?"

"To keep Jakob from playing against me?" Florence asked.

"Or to keep him from hearing what we threatened to tell him. Wilbur wants us to believe Jakob is closer to him than he is to his father."

"He is Lorenz's son. I will not harm him."

CHAPTER
TWENTY-TWO

The meeting took place at the library the next Wednesday as planned. Vivien told Lorenz about his father appearing to her and Florence.

"Father loves Jakob more than he ever loved me," he said. "Jakob could convince him to play against her if anyone can, but he loves his grandfather. I don't want him to know... we mustn't tell him about..."

"You don't want Jakob to know about his killing Florence? Or that he would do anything to win?"

"Neither."

"Can you think of any way to convince Jakob to play against Florence?"

"What would that solve?"

"I'm thinking it might make Wilbur decide to play against her himself. Would that convince him?"

"I don't know. Why would Jakob play against a ghost? He would need to know at least some of what happened all those years ago. He can't know everything. I won't allow it."

Vivien stared at the chess board set up between them. She

suddenly felt her youth and inexperience. There must be a way to convince Wilbur to sit across from Florence in the final game.

"I guess . . ." she began. "I don't know how to do this." Tears of frustration gathered in her eyes, and she brushed at them with her fingers. As young as she was, she had the words needed, but how could she put them together to convince either Jakob or Wilbur to play a game against a ghost? If she convinced Jakob, she believed his grandfather would insist on taking his place.

She told Lorenz that Jakob would have to be convinced, or they would both let Florence down. "She can't rest until this is done."

He shook his head.

"You loved her. She still loves you. She's asked me for my help. We can speak to your son together."

"I can't —" Lorenz began.

"He doesn't need to know about the murder. He doesn't need to know anything except that the game was never played in 1910, and fifty years later the ghost of one of the players needs to finish it. I think I can convince Florence to show herself to him."

Lorenz said nothing for a while, then nodded. "Where will we meet for this game?"

"The school auditorium."

"How will we get in?"

"Florence can take care of that."

They set the date for Sunday when fewer people would be in the area. At 11:00 in the morning, most people would be in church.

"How can I let you know if he won't come?" Lorenz asked.

"I guess you just won't show up."

He nodded and touched the white king. They'd switched

sides as part of the show of his teaching her to play. She helped clear the board.

Florence appeared after dark, and Vivien told her the plan. "You may have to show yourself to Jakob. If he decides to play, we hope his grandfather will be tempted to replace him. Lorenz said you can beat Jakob. His grandfather must know that, too."

∽

Florence had no trouble with the door lock. Vivien waited outside on the steps. The only worry came when a Killeen City police car drove by. The officer never looked her way. Lorenz didn't arrive until ten past. He parked in one of the metered spaces on the opposite side of the street and walked across, carrying a chess set in a box. Jakob followed, clearly reluctant to be there.

No one else was visible on the street. Vivien turned toward the door, which opened on its own. Jakob looked surprised to see no one inside who could have opened the door. "How did you . . ." Vivien led them into the foyer without answering. The door into the auditorium opened by itself. His eyes got big, and he stopped. "I know you said a ghost wanted to . . . I don't like this."

Lorenz spoke to his son in soft words Vivien couldn't quite hear. One of the tables sat near the stage with a chair on each side. Lorenz set the box on the table, opened it, and took out the board. He removed the pieces, placing them in their positions.

Vivien and Jakob watched as if mesmerized by every movement. Jakob turned to her and asked, "Are you the ghost?"

"No," she said, surprised by the question. "I'm Vivien. Florence asked me to help her arrange this game." She touched the amulet she'd put on just before leaving home. It was warm, maybe from the heat of the day.

"What connection do you have to her?"

"None."

"Then why did you agree to do this? I mean, you must believe she's real."

"It's a long story. And yes, she's real." She looked around, hoping Florence had appeared. There was no sign of her. "Florence, we're here," she called out.

"We're ready," Lorenz said. He looked around, too. "Since she's not showing herself, I guess you might as well make the choice." He held out his closed hands, each holding one of the kings.

"This is crazy," Jakob said.

"Choose," his father said.

Jakob tapped his father's left hand. Lorenz opened it to reveal the black king.

"Florence will play white."

His voice broke, and Vivien remembered he had not yet seen Florence. Why hadn't she shown herself?

A rustling sound from the direction of the door made her turn. Florence walked toward them. She wore a different dress than before, a blue print fabric with a high neckline. Vivien recognized it as the one she wore when she played the semifinal game in the tournament, but without the hole made by the knife.

Lorenz gasped and whispered her name. When she stopped near them, he reached toward her. She drew back.

"You haven't changed," he said.

"You have."

"I'm older."

"And I hope, wiser," she said.

He nodded.

She walked to the table opposite Jakob, who stood in front of his chair. She nodded to her opponent and sat down.

"You can't be a ghost." Jakob dropped into the chair.

Florence reached out a hand as if inviting him to shake hands. He responded tentatively, then jerked back when their fingertips touched.

"She's so cold," he said, looking up at his father.

Lorenz stared at the young woman he had loved. His face had gone white. Only his eyes moved as he shifted his gaze from his son to his beloved.

"Florence, when you're ready," Vivien said. The ghost moved a pawn forward.

Jakob stared at the chessboard. "I can't do this."

"You can," Lorenz said. "For your grandfather. For me. Finish it."

"What if I lose?"

"We all lose sometimes. If you do, it's because she played better than you today. There's no shame in that."

Lorenz looked over at Vivien, where she now sat on his left. She nodded. "Give them both peace," she said. "Your grandfather and Florence. It's been too long." She wondered how much Lorenz had told his son about what happened fifty years ago.

Jakob wiped at his hands with his fingertips and took a deep breath. "All right," he said. "I'm ready." He looked across at Florence, who smiled for the first time, then he concentrated on the board. He moved a pawn two squares.

The door slammed open with a bang that echoed through the auditorium. Everyone turned to see Wilbur Foxe stride toward them, his lips curled in anger.

"Stop this nonsense," he yelled.

"Grandfather?" Jakob leapt up and cried out.

Vivien exhaled loudly and nodded.

Lorenz looked at the ghost of his father with an unreadable expression on his face. It looked partly angry, partly sad, mixed with relief. And something else.

Florence smiled in satisfaction. Fear sent chills through Vivien's body. Did Florence want more than she said?

CHAPTER
TWENTY-THREE

Wilbur reached the table and stared down at his grandson.

"Are you going to play against her?" Jakob asked.

"None of us will play against her," Wilbur said.

"One of us has to," Lorenz said. "You'll never be at peace if you don't."

"I am at peace."

"If you are, why have you come?" Lorenz asked. "Why aren't you in hell where you belong?"

Father and son looked at each other long and hard. Lorenz dropped his gaze first.

"If you hadn't thought you loved her, none of this would have happened," Wilbur said.

"Don't blame me. You didn't kill her because I loved her." Lorenz looked from his father to his son, realizing he had blurted out what he never wanted Jakob to know.

"Grandfather?" Jakob said.

"Leave the table, Jakob," Wilbur said.

"You play me or Jakob does," Florence said. She still sat, looking at him with unshakable calm.

"You think you can —"

"I can strike him down in the blink of an eye." She glanced at Jakob.

Wilbur raised a fist in impotent rage. Did Florence have some sort of super strength, more than he did? Was he afraid?

"I won't let you harm him," Wilbur said, his fist still raised. His voice shook, either with rage or fear.

"Then you should not have come," Florence said. "The game has begun." She returned her attention to the chess board. Before anyone could say anything else, she attacked with her bishop.

Jakob righted his chair and sat. Everyone watched until he reached for his knight.

"No." Wilbur stepped forward and grabbed Jakob's wrist. Grandfather and grandson locked gazes until Jakob rose from the chair and stepped aside.

"Did you kill her?" he asked as Wilbur released his wrist.

Wilbur sat in the chair and scooted closer to the table. Vivien guessed he'd recognized the gambit Florence played and knew the defense.

"Yes," Wilbur said.

"Because she's a woman?" Jakob asked.

"No woman ever won the tournament." Wilbur looked up at his grandson. "That was reason enough."

Did Jakob agree? His closeness to his grandfather could mean he shared his prejudices.

Tears streaked down Lorenz's cheeks. For what happened so many years ago?

Wilbur defended with his knight, and Florence moved another pawn. He looked puzzled by her move. Vivien wondered how this could possibly end well.

The game progressed slowly, every move considered. The sound of the clock on the wall drew Vivien's attention, and she watched the pendulum swing with each tick. She returned her attention to the game, wishing she understood what was happening. The players' expressions gave no clue as to who had the advantage. Nor did the other two observers. Not even a hint as to whom each of them supported, although only Jakob's alliance was a mystery.

The room grew hotter. The doors had to be closed so no one would suspect they were inside. Vivien wanted to go to the small kitchen and see if any drinks had been left in the refrigerator but couldn't bring herself to rise from the chair. Sweat ran down her sides, making her shiver. Another glance at the clock showed it was only half past 12:00.

The games in the tournament mostly lasted an hour, give or take fifteen minutes. How long would this one take? Both players had more at stake than the tournament players. So did the two men watching.

The game went on, neither side seeming to gain an advantage. When Wilbur moved his pawn, Vivien stood.

"We need a break."

Lorenz and Jakob looked up, blinking as if waking from a trance. The son stood and stretched. "I could use some water."

He went out to the metal water fountain in the foyer and drank deeply. Vivien followed while Lorenz went to find a men's room. She waited while Jakob drank. He straightened and wiped his mouth with the back of his hand.

"Do you believe Grandfather killed her?" he asked.

"Yes, I do."

"Why? I know he's prejudiced, but . . . she was young and couldn't possibly have beaten him."

"Are you watching the game in there?" Vivien nodded

toward the auditorium. "She's giving him a run for his money as far as I can tell."

"Yes..."

"Your father said she could have beaten him."

"He hates Grandfather."

"Why do you think that is?"

She went to the water fountain, then followed Jakob into the auditorium. Reaching her chair, she stretched both arms overhead and sat down. Lorenz soon followed. The players sat still, studying the board. With a nod, Florence moved her rook toward her king to protect him.

They jockeyed for position. The next time Vivien looked at the clock, it was 1:15. They couldn't possibly stay much longer in the auditorium. She couldn't stay away from home, either. Her parents were expecting her well before supper. What excuse could she give? If only she could get to a phone and call them. What would she say? Her friend wanted her to stay longer? Maybe overnight? Compounding the lie?

Please, don't let the game last much longer.

CHAPTER
TWENTY-FOUR

It ended suddenly. Wilbur moved his remaining knight, leaving the queen vulnerable. Florence moved her bishop, attacking his queen and leaving the king exposed. It seemed obvious, even to a non-player.

Wilbur refused to yield and shuffled pieces. He couldn't save his king.

"The game is rigged," he shouted.

Florence opened her mouth to respond, but Lorenz stood and cut her off.

"How, Father? How is it rigged?" He waved a hand at the board. "You've done all you could and Florence won."

"She can't win. Not against me." Wilbur turned to his grandson. "You saw it. You know. Her game was sloppy. Unorganized."

"Grandfather, it's over. You lost this time. Next time —"

"There won't be a next time," Florence said. "It's done. The last game has been played."

"No!"

"Father, it's over," Lorenz said. "Florence won."

Wilbur looked over at Vivien. His eyes seemed to blaze. A trick of the light? "You." He spat out the word. "This is your doing. You brought this on us." He lunged at her.

Vivien backed up and grasped the amulet. Before he reached her, Florence stepped between them. She waved a hand, but Vivien saw several hands. Or maybe she saw the hand move in slow motion, sort of like those books with a series of pictures. When you fanned the pages, the figure appeared to move. However it was, Wilbur stumbled backward.

The ghost of the young woman moved swiftly to stand in front of the man she once loved. He was an old man, while she still looked the same as at the time of her death. Lorenz gazed at her uplifted face.

"I loved you so." Tears glistened in his eyes and on his cheeks.

"Yet you let him murder me," she said.

"He was . . . is . . . my father. I didn't think he would go so far."

Her right hand lashed out and grabbed him by the throat. "I died while you watched."

His hands grabbed at hers, finding nothing to take hold of. He slapped at his throat, gasping for air.

"Florence," Vivien cried out. "Don't." She grabbed hold of the amulet on its cord around her neck and started toward her.

Jakob tried to push Florence away. The ghost had become air and light. "Please," he begged.

"Florence," Vivien nearly whispered. "He loved you. He still loves you." Still holding onto the amulet, she reached toward Florence. She felt the energy, the anger leave the ghost.

Slowly Florence released Lorenz. He crumpled to the floor, coughing and trying to breathe. No one rushed to him. Instead, they watched Florence walk toward the exit.

Wilbur was also gone. He'd disappeared while everyone concentrated on Florence.

While Lorenz sat on the floor catching his breath, Jakob packed up the chess set and closed the box.

Vivien wondered about... many things. Maybe she'd made a mistake this time in trusting the ghost of Florence. She'd seemed so nice, hurt, and only wanting to finish what she'd started. In the end, had she also wanted revenge? Not against Wilbur, but against Lorenz. No, that desire was not the driving force behind her return. Otherwise, Lorenz would be dead, too.

She followed Jakob and Lorenz out of the auditorium and through the main doorway onto the sidewalk. The two men got into the car at the curb, and Vivien walked in the direction of the bus station.

CHAPTER
TWENTY-FIVE

Daddy questioned Vivien when she got home and grounded her for not getting home when she should have and not calling to let them know. Mama saw how tired and upset she was and sent her to her room, as if it were punishment.

She fell asleep until supper was ready. Afterward, the four of them sat in the living room, the lights dim, and watched *Maverick*. She went out to the picnic table. The sky overhead was hazy and only the brightest stars were visible.

"My father always said we can't trust white men," Florence said. "He was right."

Startled, Vivien sat up. "I thought you were gone."

"Soon."

"Was your father with you in the auditorium? Did you count on his strength combined with yours to overcome Wilbur? To keep him from hurting anyone?"

"He would not let him hurt me again. Both of us can rest now."

Vivien nodded. "You told me you weren't after revenge."

"When I stood close to Lorenz, my feelings got all mixed up. Anger became so strong, I couldn't..."

"He's paid for not saving you every day since."

"Maybe. But my father was right."

"You trusted me," Vivien pointed out. "You also saved me."

Florence began to fade. "Thank you."

Vivien lay back down on the tabletop. Tears ran from the corners of her eyes toward her ears, tickling, and she wiped at them. Sitting up again, she let the tears flow. Florence was the second close friend she'd lost in two years.

The memory of Mignon ached inside her. Although she and Florence had not been as close, she would miss her. The intimacy she shared with both girls was stronger than any other she'd experienced. Except perhaps for her mother and sister. She still had them.

Vivien found a tissue in the pocket of her shorts. She blew her nose and wiped away the tears with her hands. She climbed down and went inside to watch whatever TV show Daddy had decided on.

Two weeks later, Jack called and asked if she would meet him at the movies on Saturday. When she asked how he got her number, he told her that Mrs. Stirling gave it to him, without explaining why his former teacher did that. They began meeting at various places in Killeen while he waited until he turned 18 when his father promised to get him a car.

After school started in the fall, Daddy announced he was being sent to Korea in January. The family would have to stay stateside, either in Tennessee with Grandma again, or in Harker Heights. Vivien got her wish when Mama chose to stay in Texas.

Months passed without another ghost appearing. Maybe it was because they didn't move to a new place. Vivien was glad of the respite and concentrated on her studies. Jack applied to several colleges. Vivien wished more than anything that she could apply to West Point or the Air Force Academy, but they didn't accept women.

The counselor at school hinted that she didn't really need to go to college to find a husband. Why would a woman with a college education assume that was all Vivien wanted? The real problem was the lack of money. Even if she got an after-school-job, there would never be enough.

Adults always asked boys what they wanted to be when they grew up. Most adults assumed girls dreamed of a husband and children.

Were there women lawyers? That was what she found interesting. She'd loved Perry Mason on TV, although being a lawyer wasn't really anything like they portrayed it. Still, studying the law appealed to her. She'd have to find a way.

In the meantime, she studied and got good grades. When she turned 16 Mama and Daddy agreed she could date Jack, after they met him, although Daddy thought he was too old for her.

The summer grew hotter. Lauren fell out with Sylvia and turned to Vivien for comfort. The trips to the library continued, and they looked forward to next spring when school was out.

[LOCATIONS ARE SET where I remember them in 1960 or where online research places them.]

About the Author

Cary Herwig is an author of middle grade/young adult horror fiction. This is the second book in *The Army Brat Hauntings* series and Cary's thirteenth published book. You can find Cary's blog at https://caryosbornewriter.blogspot.com/ and email her at iroshiok@gmail.com.

Also by Cary Osborne

The Army Brat Hauntings

The Ghost's Daughter

The World Ends at the River

Friends Like Dust